D1711497

THE CHRISTMAS PRESENT

AN ABSOLUTELY ADDICTIVE PSYCHOLOGICAL THRILLER FULL OF SHOCKING TWISTS

LORNA DOUNAEVA

Copyright © 2024 by Lorna Dounaeva

All rights reserved.

No portion of this book may be reproduced in any form without written permission from the publisher or author, except as permitted by U.S. copyright law.

PROLOGUE

THE CAR REACTS TO my slightest touch, as if we are one. I have never felt so happy, so high. Even though there are two other cars ahead of me, I know I've got this. I take the next corner, one eye on the road, the other on my competitors. Shelby's car tilts slightly and comes up on two wheels. Then it's turning, spinning towards Tina. Tina takes evasive action, but it's too late. Shelby's car is shunting her off the road.

An explosion rocks the air. Shards of metal and burning debris fly in all directions. A scream rips through my skull as I watch both cars burst into flames. The smoke is like a blizzard. My eyes water, and I feel a wave of terror and heat. I'm coming up on them fast. I have to do something, anything, to stop myself from hitting them. I press the accelerator harder, forcing the car so high up the wall it almost flips. My arms turn like crazy, making a U-turn away from the fireball. There are more cars heading my way now. I am skidding left, then right, avoiding each oncoming vehicle. I hear the impact as more cars pile up, but I keep on driving. I can't afford to lose concentration.

I have to get through this.

I have to get home to my family.

ONE

TAYLOR

LUCY FLICKS OUT HER blue tongue, laughing and talking at the same time.

I take a big gulp of my slushie and show her mine, shuddering with brain freeze.

I notice a younger girl blatantly staring at us with her piercing brown eyes. She has a purple streak that weaves through her wavy black hair. Looking at her, I think of my little sister, Clara, who used to stare at me like that so she could mimic my every move. But this girl looks older than Clara, and she seems to have no clue about personal space. I stare back at her, waiting for her to blink, but she doesn't.

I nudge Lucy, who gives her a look, and we walk past her, tossing our empty cups into the recycling bin as we head into H&M.

'They're having a sale!' Lucy shrieks, a bit too loud.

I catch the amused look of the shop assistant. Lucy is a bit overexcited but they haven't had a sale since August. It feels like forever. We grab armfuls of clothes and head to the fitting room, where we spend the next twenty minutes trying on different outfits.

'I love these red trousers,' I say, admiring the way they fit. 'But I'm never going to wear them.'

'They do look great on you,' Lucy says, snapping a picture with her phone. 'Let's save this. If we put a decent background on it, you can put it on Instagram.'

We leave the changing rooms, and stop to take the piss out of some of the festive items on display; reindeer antlers, musical earrings, and worse still, a white snowman dress with a knitted orange carrot poking out of it.

'You know you want to buy that,' Lucy whispers to me.

'I would, but you're going to buy it first.'

She shrieks with laughter as I steer her over to the till. We pay for our purchases, none of which includes the snowman dress. As we turn to leave the shop. I spot the same young girl from earlier. Her arms are crossed, and her eyes are narrowed. She's a little older than I thought before, maybe ten, but the look on her face is just as unnerving.

The shopping centre is decked in tinsel, and there's another Christmas tree every few metres. The whole place smells of mince pies and corny Christmas music is playing on the speakers. It's doing my head in. Lucy dances beside me, humming along to the tunes.

'I'm so getting into the Christmas spirit,' she says.

'All this Christmas stuff is just there to mess with us. To make us hand over our money.'

She looks at me and smiles. 'Well, it's worked, hasn't it?'

I look down at my shopping bags. I suppose she's right.

There is a grotto set up in the middle of the shopping centre, and little kids are queuing up to see Father Christmas. I find it quite funny. I mean, there are grown adults dressed in elf costumes. They are all way too big to be elves and I happen to know one of them is Phoebe Barman's dad. Everyone at school knows it's him, but she won't admit it.

'Have you got time to go to the bookshop?' I say hopefully.

Lucy consults her phone. 'Can't be long. I don't want to miss my bus.'

'I just need a quick look,' I promise.

We walk upstairs, past a couple of security guards in their uniforms. They look at us as we pass. I feel my cheeks flame as Lucy blows them a kiss.

'Lucy! They're like thirty!'

Lucy giggles. 'Do a whistle.'

'No!'

'Go on, you're better at it than me.'

'Lucy!'

'Don't be a chicken.'

Oh my god, she's not going to shut up.

She screws up her face and lets out a long wolf-whistle, then we run around the corner, laughing and panting to get our breath back. I hope to god they don't think that was me.

Lucy has her phone out. She's scrolling as she walks.

'Here, have you seen this?' she asks.

She shows me a video of some mums in our local park, pushing kids in buggies and holding signs that say *'Make Our Parks Safe Again'* and *'Knife Amnesty Now.'* The park looks the same as always: worn paths, litter scattered near the bins, and a group of kids kicking a football against the graffiti-covered wall. One of the mums speaks directly to the camera, her voice sharp and urgent, as the others march behind her.

'We are taking our park back. This space is for kids to play in, and for people to jog in or walk their dogs. Starting today, we are going to be doing regular citizen patrols to make sure this park remains for local people. No more crime on our doorstep.'

The mums behind her work themselves into a frenzy, chanting the last line and everybody cheers. A few passers-by glance over but keep walking, and the camera pans slowly away, following a jogger as he finishes his lap around the park.

'Embarrassing,' I say, handing her phone back.

Lucy slips it back into her pocket and we walk on. The little bell tinkles as I push open the door to Pemberly Pages and step inside, taking in a deep gulp of air. I love that smell, a heady combination of freshly printed paper, worn leather and a hint of dust. Lucy trails behind me as I make a beeline for the graphic novels.

My fingers trace books with hauntingly beautiful covers featuring ghosts and vampires. I was hoping there would be something new, but I've got all of these already.

'Are you getting anything?' Lucy asks, sounding bored. She gave up reading when she was twelve. I've tried to convince her she just needs to find the right book, but she totally lost interest after our English teacher made us read The

Scarlet Letter. I'm not one of those crazy book banners, but maybe there's a case for that one.

We walk out and head towards the exit. I notice a group of girls loitering nearby. They don't go to our school, but they look kind of…hard. There are about six of them. The youngest might be about Year Seven, the oldest Year Twelve, practically grown up. They all have dark, emo hair that hangs across their faces like curtains. The oldest one stands out with her razor-thin eyebrows. Eyes set a little too far apart. Most of them are covered in piercings—noses, lips, ears, even one with a stud on her cheek. One of them has a tattoo of thorns spiralling around her collarbone. The dark ink is sharp against her pale skin.

Then I see her. The girl with the purple streak in her hair. She doesn't look as emo as the others, but she's definitely part of their group. She sees me too, and as we lock eyes, my stomach flips. They fall dead silent as we walk past. I pick up my pace, bursting out the door and into the car park. They are right behind us. I shoot a panicked glance at Lucy. I don't think she's even noticed, but she can be a bit slow on the uptake. I nudge her with my elbow. We keep moving, but I risk a look over my shoulder at them. They are walking towards us. Their hushed voices grow louder as they trail us, and I can feel the tension rising in my chest.

'Do you know them?' I whisper.

'Never seen them before.'

We pick up our pace, almost jogging along now. My heart races as my mind scrambles for an escape plan. The car park is empty. There's no one around and we're outnumbered two to eight.

A voice cuts through the air, loud and taunting:

'Where do you think you're going?'

I glance down at my smartwatch and dial.

'Mum, come quickly. We're near the bus station and some nasty girls are chasing us.'

I keep going. I don't even wait for her reply. We reach the grimy concrete steps and head out onto the high street. I've never been so happy to see people. Lucy and I dart forward, weaving in and out of the crowds.

I'm thinking hard. We need to get to the bus station. I'm hoping Mum will be there soon, ready to pick us up. But we don't want that lot following us. We need to lose them.

'I know a shortcut,' Lucy says.

She takes a left into a side road. I hear a low whistle and know without looking that they are still there.

Lucy takes the next right, heading up an alley between two buildings. There's a stink, like rancid fish as we weave between stacks of crates and overflowing bins. Hot vapour billows out of a heating duct. I follow Lucy through the narrow alley. Even though it's broad daylight, I'm starting to get creeped out. My shopping bags weigh me down, and I can barely squeeze through, but Lucy keeps going.

As we round the corner, Lucy points up at street level.

'That's my bus!'

She leaps over the fence like Catwoman. I try to follow, but it's difficult in my heeled boots. My bag gets caught between the fence posts and I stumble backwards, landing hard on my ankle.

'Lucy!' I yell after her.

But she's already gone.

The voices are getting louder. I pick out a few of the words they are saying: 'Get the skank! Don't let her go!'

I wince in pain and the youngest girl, the one that was staring at me earlier, softens her expression. She holds out her hand and starts to help me up, but then she pulls her hand away suddenly, and I fall back down, banging my head.

For a moment, everything goes funky. I feel like I'm in a pool. Their faces swim in front of me. Their features press themselves into my brain. One looks like a beaver with bucked teeth. Another has chronic acne, covered up with those little blue star patches you buy in Superdrug. They could get me. They could grab me right now, but instead they all stare at me, snarling like dogs. I see the hate in their eyes and it's freaking me out.

My head is banging as I climb to my feet. I don't go the way Lucy went. The youngest girl is so close to me I can smell her onion breath on my face. She leans closer and gnashes her teeth like she's going to bite me. I take off, running round the side of the building, praying there's another way out, but as I reach the end of the of the alley, I see it's blocked. Nothing but a big brick wall.

She is barking at me like a dog.

'Woof! Woof!'

The others are just behind. They bark too. Loud and fierce. The noise jars my ears and my stupid legs are shaking.

I spot a window above the wheelie bins. It's open just a crack. I reach up and throw it open. I throw my bags inside, then I heave myself up and clamber in after them.

The girl grabs my legs. I'm kicking and she's pulling. I'm wriggling like crazy, my arms searching for the floor, my legs trying to shake her off.

'What the hell?'

A man appears in front of me. 'What on earth do you think you're doing?'

'Help me!'

I don't see his face, but I think he goes to the window and looks down.

'You lot! Out!'

I kick hard. I think I get her. Then she pulls off my boot, or maybe one of the others does. I fall on my face and a moment later, I hear the window slam. It's the man who's shut it. I look up at him, dazed.

'Thanks!'

'You can't be in here,' he says gruffly. I sit up and look around. I'm in the gent's toilets. The man goes to the sink and washes his hands. He's wearing an apron and a chef's hat.

I grab my bags and walk out. I'm walking funny because of my missing boot. I head down a corridor, past a kitchen, out into a restaurant. There are people sitting there eating, posh music playing. The air stinks of garlic. Someone taps on the window. Everyone looks over. The girl is there, holding up my boot. She waves it about, as if we're mates, and this is some big joke.

I shoot past the diners, hopping along. I come out into a small reception area. I head to the door and peer outside. There's no sign of them, but they must be out there somewhere. Is it safe? Maybe I should go back the way I came, through the loos, down into the alley again. They won't be expecting that. They won't...

My phone beeps. That'll be Mum, trying to call me. Or Lucy wondering where I am.

'Woof!'

My shoulders tense. My nose runs.

I turn slowly, willing myself to look at them.

The door flies open, and something comes flying at me. Hits me in the mouth.

My boot.

I grab it, blood dripping from my lip.

I push past them and run down the road. My heart is pounding. The girls are after me, laughing, barking. Louder and louder. I run, arms flailing. Somewhere along the line, I've lost my shopping bags, but I don't care. I just have to make it to the bus station.

To Mum.

TWO

JOY

THE BOY RACERS REV their engines, the guttural roar bouncing off the surrounding buildings as they wait for the lights to change. Their car is a Volkswagen Golf GTI. It looks ordinary at first glance, but I can tell they've put some work into it. I feel the spark pulsing through my veins. I understand the urge to race, the excitement, the electricity. I check out the driver and see the eagerness in his eye. He's sitting forward in his seat, anxious to get going. His friends are cheering, eager. Their music is pumping.

My fingers tingle with the urge to rev my own engine, but I'm a respectable wife and mum now. People depend on me. I can't... Oh God, he's revving his engine. I know I shouldn't, but I open the window just a crack and inhale the fumes.

The music is pumping, faster and faster, sending us all into a frenzy. The lads appear to have clocked me. Perhaps they've spotted the fire in my eye. They're checking out my motor. The driver is revving his engine again. As the lights change to amber, my phone rings, and I answer using Bluetooth.

Taylor's voice sounds breathless: 'Mum, come quickly. We're near the bus station and some nasty girls are chasing us.'

I feel as if the breath has been knocked out of me.

'Taylor? Who's chasing you? What the hell's happening?'

But there's no reply.

The seatbelt feels too tight across my chest. My eyes flick left to right. I roll the window down a little more so I can breathe. Then I square my shoulders and check the road. 'Mum's coming!'

I slam my foot on the accelerator just as the lights change and roar away. I hear the squeal of my tires, the indignant shrieks of the lads as I leave them to eat my dust.

'Taylor? Taylor! Are you still there?'

My fingers tap against the steering wheel in rhythm with my racing heart. Normally I would drive through the centre of town, but that road will be congested. I take a sharp left. It all looks clear. I turn again, zooming around other vehicles, eyes peeled for movement on the pavements. You never quite know when someone's going to leap out in front of you. One more turn and I spot a large removal van. My foot hovers over the brake. Two men are perched on the back, drinking tea. I keep going, picking up speed as I approach another set of lights. They're already on amber. I floor it, screeching through as the lights change to red. There's the multi-storey up ahead.

My heart lurches as I spot Taylor running along, her blonde hair flying behind her. She's limping slightly, favouring her right leg as a pack of feral girls pursue her.

Not just girls. A couple of them are older teenagers, almost adult. I shoot past them all and skid to a halt a few meters up the road. Taylor runs to the car and dives into the passenger seat. She hasn't even got the door closed when something smacks into the roof, causing the whole car to vibrate.

A coke can slides down the window, spraying fizzy brown liquid as it rolls off the bonnet and bounces into the gutter. It leaves a sticky mess down the front windscreen. I'm lucky it didn't smash the window.

I grip the steering wheel tightly, boiling with rage. How dare they? Every instinct screams at me to reverse back into them. That would teach them to mess with us! But I resist. Instead, I blare my horn. They don't even flinch as we zoom away.

'What the hell?' I say, watching as the girls disappear in the rearview mirror. There's something very unsettling about the way they stand in the road like that, like they have no fear at all. And the oldest one... the oldest one really ought to know better. She's much too old to be behaving like this, hounding young girls with her gang of thugs.

The car beeps impatiently as Taylor slides on her seatbelt. I check the road and join the queue of traffic, heading back toward our house.

'Do they go to your school?' I ask.

'No. I've never seen them before.'

I draw a deep breath and glance at my firstborn. 'So what happened?'

'I don't know.'

'You must have some idea?'

'I was shopping with Lucy when one of them started following us, and before I knew it, there was a whole crowd.'

'Where is Lucy?'

'I think she got on the bus. I was right behind her, but I fell.'

'Call her, check she's alright.'

I head toward the bridge as Taylor taps out a message on her phone. A few seconds later, there's a ping.

'She's fine, Mum. She's halfway home.'

'Good.'

I release the tension in my shoulders. 'Are you alright?'

Taylor folds her arms over her chest. 'Oh yeah, I'm just great.'

I bite my lip. 'What exactly happened? Did they say anything?'

Taylor looks out the window. 'I already told you. They were following me.'

I shoot her a look. 'Are you sure you didn't do anything?'

'Why do you always assume everything's my fault?'

'I don't. I just want to get to the bottom of it, that's all.'

She falls silent, and I can see she's still upset. But my gut feeling is that something is off here. Taylor's been different lately, stroppy and unpredictable, throwing her weight around the house. Perhaps she looked at one of them the wrong way. But really, who behaves like that? Chasing down a couple of strangers? They were clearly outnumbered. I don't even want to think about what might have happened if they had caught them.

She doesn't say anything more as I drive toward Clara's school.

'Oh god, do we have to?' she groans as we roll into the car park.

'Yes, we have to collect Clara.'

Taylor slides down in her seat as I find a space. My youngest daughter has stayed behind for nativity rehearsals. She has the very important job of being The Star. She's very proud of the role. She has to wear a big gold costume, which is shiny and glittery and completely over the top, much like her.

'Can I stay in the car?' Taylor asks.

'If you want. Unless you'd like a look at your old school?'

She pulls a face. 'I saw enough of it when I was there, thanks.'

'Suit yourself.' I linger for a moment. 'Maybe you'd like to give Dad a call?'

She looks at me like I've suggested peeling the nails off her fingers. 'Why?'

'Well, you know. He's a good listener.'

And there's a chance he might be able to get more out of her, in his calm, gentle way.

Taylor pulls her knees up to her chest and disappears into her collar like a turtle.

'Just shut up, will you? Stop making a big deal out of it.'

I let out a puff of air. I don't know if I want to hug her or slap her. 'Have it your own way,' I say, climbing out of the car.

She doesn't even wait for me to get out. She's already whacked up her music. It's awful wailing and whining, blasting out of the windows. It doesn't even have a beat.

As I walk across the playground, I blink back a few tears. Everyone warned me about teenagers, but I never thought it would be this hard. This... creature I've just left in the car is nothing like the sweet little girl who used to hold my hand and skip along beside me.

Nothing like Clara.

I head towards the hall where Clara is finishing the last number. I'm not supposed to have seen any of it yet, so I make sure she doesn't see me peeking. But they've had a few of these rehearsals over the last couple of weeks, and I can't help but catch the tune and pick up the lyrics. It's a catchy number, and I find myself humming along as Clara sings in her sweet voice:

'The shepherds and their woolly sheep
are all so glad you came.
Jesus and the three wise men
all hope you'll come again.
From the angels and the innkeeper,
and the star that twinkled bright.
A heavenly Christmas, one and all.
The little donkey says "Goodnight".'

A pantomime donkey clip-clops across the stage, leaving Mary and Joseph alone in the stable. Without missing a beat, Mary shoves the baby Jesus doll into Joseph's arms. Joseph takes one look at him and shoves him in the crib, then they both reach for the pile of presents heaped in front of them.

'Thank you, everybody, for coming!' Clara says into the mic. 'Please donate kindly to the fund to fix the school roof! Before you head off, I want to thank Mrs Postlethwaite and all the other teachers and the mums and dads that have helped to make this year's show our best production yet!'

In Clara's little voice, the word *production* sounds so big. Clara is very small for her age. So small, I had to take her to the doctor for tests. She is the tiniest child in her year. In fact, she's smaller than some of the Reception kids.

Luckily, Clara has a big enough personality that it isn't a problem, socially at least. Nobody would dare accuse her of being a baby. She's just a very small child who will most likely grow up to be a very small adult.

Once she has finished, Clara hops down off the stage and flounces over to me.

'You weren't listening, were you?'

I throw my hands up. 'No, of course not! Wouldn't dream of it!'

Clara's teacher, Mrs Postlethwaite, is smirking at me. 'Am I alright to take her home now?' I ask.

'Please do! Unless Clara would like to go and change first?'

There is zero point in asking Clara if she wants to change out of her star outfit and back into her very ordinary school uniform.

We walk towards the car, and she climbs into her booster seat in the back, complaining again that Taylor is allowed to sit in the front.

'When you're my age, you can sit in the front,' Taylor says.

'No, because you'll still be there,' Clara retorts. 'Forever and ever and ever.'

'She might leave home at some point,' I say.

Clara shakes her head. 'I doubt it.'

I reach over and change the music to something more soothing. Taylor shoots me a poisonous look and turns to look out the window.

Clara pulls her dolls out of her backpack. There is a school rule about not bringing in toys from home. Clara flaunts it daily and I don't stop her. You have to pick your battles.

'What's for dinner?' Clara asks, as she takes out a brush and begins styling her blue-haired doll.

'I was thinking of spaghetti and meatballs,' I say.

Clara cheers. Taylor groans.

I pull into our drive. Clara twists in her seat.

'Is Daddy home?'

'I expect so.'

She shoves her dolls back in her bag and bursts through the door, yelling at the top of her voice:

'Daddy, I'm home! Daddy!'

'I'd better make sure she takes that damned costume back into school,' I mutter.

Taylor nods, but I can see she's not listening.

'You alright, love?'

She hunches her shoulders. 'Of course!'

'I was thinking about those girls earlier...'

'Yeah, well, we're home now. No need to go on about it. Don't say anything to Dad, will you?'

'Why not?'

'It's embarrassing.'

I don't make any promises, but I understand. Everything is embarrassing at Taylor's age.

We head inside. The house is silent. I pop my head into the study. Howard is working, deep in concentration, as he stares at his spreadsheets. There's something adorable about how much he loves his work.

I leave him to it and head to the kitchen to make a start on dinner. The meatballs are ready-made, so all it requires from me is to pop open the jar of sauce, throw in a few veggies and boil water for the spaghetti.

Howard joins me just as I'm nibbling on a big hunk of cheese. He's wearing a suit, even though he's been working from home. He always looks smart, but right now his tie is askew and he has a blue ink stain on the pocket of his shirt.

'Finished the end-of-year report!'

'Well done!'

He looks at me. 'How was your day?'

'The usual,' I say.

I was in the office today, while he worked from home. We take it in turns, because there is only one good workspace here and we both find it more productive.

I consider telling him about Taylor's run in with those girls, but he is already popping open the wine and pouring two glasses to celebrate his accomplishment. I can't rain on his parade.

We eat in the kitchen. Clara monopolises the conversation, chattering on about the nativity while Taylor pushes the meatballs around her plate.

'Not hungry?' I ask.

'No, I had something at Riverwood.'

Howard takes his glasses off and polishes them on his tie. 'Got much homework?'

'For goodness' sake, Dad! I can manage my own homework. You don't have to badger me.'

We exchange a look, but let it slide.

Clara plays with her teeth. 'Something wrong, love?'

'I've got a wobbly one.'

'Oh, is it sore?'

'A little bit, but I don't want it to fall out.'

Howard looks up from his dinner. 'It's got to fall out sometime, hasn't it?'

Clara looks at him. 'No, I need to keep it in my mouth until Christmas Eve.'

'Why?'

Taylor's face brightens. 'So the Tooth Fairy and Father Christmas have to meet.'

'I'm sure they already know each other, don't they?' Howard says.

Clara leans forward. 'Everyone knows they hate each other.'

'Do they?'

'Well, duh! If they ever meet, there's going to be a big fight.'

Howard looks troubled. 'Do we want them to fight?'

Both Clara and Taylor nod their heads.

'If the tooth fairy knocks Santa's tooth out, she has to pay him loads of money because his teeth are really old and precious.'

'And what if Santa knocks the Tooth Fairy's tooth out?'

'Then he has to give her a present.'

'Right,' says Howard, standing up from the table. 'Well, if you don't want your tooth to fall out, I guess you don't want dessert?'

'I can eat it on the other side of my mouth,' Clara says, setting down her fork.

At bed time, Clara writes her letter to Santa. I sneak a peek. She wants more of those Bliss dolls. Surprise, surprise. She's copied out the web link for Santa. She also wants an iPhone and her own TV. The kid dreams big.

I flip the note over. On the back, she's asked for a new coffee cup for Howard, because his favourite one is chipped. My heart stirs. She's also asked for a bull-frog for Taylor. And a sports car for me, a red one with an open roof, like the one in her Bliss doll play set. Wow, she must think Santa's loaded.

I replace the paper quickly and turn as she comes out of the bathroom. She reads me a chapter of the book she's reading for school, then I tuck her in and go to check on Taylor.

Her door is closed and moody music floats out under the door. I knock and go in, trying not to grimace at the pile of shoes and underwear lying in a tangled heap on the floor.

'Do you want to go ice-skating on Saturday?' I ask.

'Yeah, okay.'

'You can invite Lucy and Star if you want. I said Clara could bring a friend.'

Taylor's face clouds over.

'I'm not friends with Star anymore.'

'Why not?'

'Because all she does is lie.'

'Oh, okay.'

I wait for her to elaborate but she doesn't say anything further.

I shrug and pull the curtains closed. Star was never really my cup of tea, anyway. A bit thoughtless and impulsive. I'd much rather my daughter hung out with well mannered Lucy.

Taylor closes her eyes and looks at the wall, signalling for me to leave. I wonder if she's still thinking about those girls at Riverwood, but I know better than to pressure her.

THREE
JOY

I SLIDE INTO BED beside Howard, who is already lying back, looking relaxed. He smiles as I settle under the duvet, his hand moving to rest on my hip.

'You've been quiet tonight,' he says, his fingers tracing small circles on my waist.

'Sorry,' I say, shifting slightly. 'Got a lot on my mind.'

He raises an eyebrow, his hand pausing. 'What's up?'

I glance at him before sitting up against the headboard. 'Something happened at the shopping centre earlier. With Taylor.'

'What kind of something?'

'There was this group of girls following Taylor and Lucy, trying to intimidate them. Lucy got away but then they went after Taylor and chased her through town. She called me to come and get her, and they were throwing things at the car as we drove off.'

Howard pushes himself upright, his frown deepening. 'What did Taylor do to upset them?'

'She says she didn't do anything. But even if she did upset them in some way, that doesn't excuse them all ganging up on her like that.'

He runs a hand through his thinning hair. 'Should we report it to the police?'

I exhale. 'I don't know. What would we tell them? I don't even have a clear description.'

Howard leans back against the headboard, his hand still on my knee. 'Then maybe it's best to leave it. The police probably won't do much without more to go on.'

I nod, but my mind races. I can't let it go. Those girls can't be allowed to act like that, terrorising people.

'Although...'

I look at him. 'What?'

'Just a thought, but Riverwood has security, right? If you're that bothered, you could go down there and have a word. See if they know who they are.'

I think this over. 'Yeah, maybe they saw something. And even if they didn't, I should let them know what happened so they can keep an eye out. Something has to be done about those girls. They're a menace.'

Howard sighs and pulls me close. 'Just be careful, okay? Don't go picking fights with teenagers.'

'Don't worry,' I say, resting my head on his shoulder. 'I just want to make sure this doesn't happen again.'

But even as I say it, my resolve hardens. I'm going to go down to Riverwood first thing in the morning. At the very least, I can get them banned. I'm going to make damned sure those girls understand that we don't tolerate that kind of behaviour around here.

FOUR
TAYLOR

'Who were those bitches?' Lucy whispers into the dark.

I glance out at the hallway. Mum never quite closes the door properly. She always leaves it that little bit open, so that a splint of light falls over my otherwise dark room.

I hold the phone to my ear while I get up and shut it properly.

'How should I know?' I whisper back.

'Freaking lunatics, weren't they? Especially that little one. I should unleash Bess on her.'

I smile. Lucy's little sister is a handful.

A blood-curdling scream echoes down the line.

'Lucy?'

'It's okay. Mum's just trying to put Bess to bed.'

'It's quite late, isn't it?'

'Yeah, she never goes down without a fight. Mum got fed up and left her to it once. When we came down in the morning, the whole house was covered in flour and she was rolling in it and making snow angels.'

'And I thought Clara was bonkers.'

'Different level of bonkers.'

'But seriously. Who were these bitches at Riverwood? They're not from our school.'

'No, and none of them were wearing uniform.'

'I can't believe you left me there.'

'I thought you were right behind me. Your bus pulled in behind mine.'

I fiddle with the satin edge of my blanket. I'm still pissed off at her for leaving me like that, but if I have a go at her, I won't have any friends left. All the same, Lucy could have run and got someone. A grown up or something. Instead she just left me to it. She doesn't even seem sorry.

'I didn't know what they were going to do. If my mum hadn't turned up right at that minute, they would have attacked me or something.'

Lucy goes quiet for a minute. 'I think we should avoid Riverwood for a while.'

'We can go to Tooting next time.'

'Yeah.'

She starts going on about what she wants for Christmas, like what happened is no big deal, and I feel a fresh surge of anger. I take my stress ball and squeeze it so hard it bursts, and then there's all this gooey stuff running down my fingers.

I stay on the line for a while. Neither of us says much. It's just nice to know she's there. I lie awake, staring up at the ceiling. I try to think about something relaxing, like sheep in a field. But all I can think about is them. The looks on their faces. The feeling of being chased.

'Taylor?'

I jerk awake, breath bursting out of me as if I've been holding it in my sleep. My phone's on my pillow. Lucy's still on the call.

'Wake up, you're going to be late for school!'

I sit up and check the time. That's strange. Mum has not come in to wake me. She probably thinks I need to learn to get myself up. Most mornings I can, but last night I fell asleep without even setting my alarm. Thank the lord for Lucy.

'You talk in your sleep,' she says.

'What?'

'You were muttering something, over and over.'

'Like what?'

'Like, "Get them off me".'

'Huh.'

'You must have been dreaming about those girls.'

'I don't remember.'

I look down at what I'm wearing. I slept in my school shirt. It looks a bit wrinkled, but it will do. I leap out of bed and my history book slides off the duvet.

'I have to finish my homework.'

'What did you get for question 7 in the end?'

'Doing it now.'

I scan the text as I wriggle on my trousers. If this were geography, I'd just ask Google, but the history teacher, Mr Fig is known for putting in trick questions to stop us doing that. It's really annoying.

My stomach rumbles like a train coming through the tunnel. I really need toast.

'I'll be back in a minute,' I tell Lucy.

I charge down the stairs like my pants are on fire.

'Morning, Dad!' I say, as I reach the kitchen. He's standing by the kettle, adjusting his tie.

'Morning, Pumpkin.'

I pull a face. Pumpkin was his name for me when I was a little kid. Sometimes he forgets I'm all grown up, and he still calls me that. I suppose I don't really mind, as long as no one overhears. He means well, but it's a bit cringe.

I throw some bread in the toaster and hop from one foot to the other, waiting for it to pop.

'You okay?' Dad asks.

'Just need to finish my homework,' I say. I can admit that to him. He's not as anal about schoolwork as Mum is.

'Anything I can help with?'

'Do you know who succeeded Queen Elizabeth 1st?'

His eyes light up as he reels off every king and queen for the last four hundred years. My toast pops and I nearly burn my hands pulling it out of the toaster.

I smother it in butter and stuff it into my mouth. All the while, dad is still going.

'Right, Dad. Got to get ready!'

'Oh, well have a nice day!' he smiles brightly, and I feel bad that I haven't got time to listen to a full potted history of the British monarchy.

I run up the stairs and scribble down the answers to questions seven, eight, and nine.

I read them back to Lucy between bites of toast.

'Wow,' she seems impressed. Her mum is yelling at Bess in the background.

'What's she done now?'

'Emptied the honey jar all over the table. It's dripping everywhere.'

Mum knocks on the door. 'Ten minutes!' she yells.

'I know!' I yell back.

I finish the rest of my homework, apply a bit of concealer, and scrape my hair back into a bun. With one last glance in the mirror, I'm down the stairs and out the door with seconds to spare.

I check my smart watch. It's a fifteen-minute walk to school, ten if I walk fast, five if I run.

I set off at a fast walk. My ankle is throbbing. I should have got Mum to write me a note for PE.

I spot someone up ahead. It's Phoebe Barman, who's always late. I pick up my pace. My ankle is still sore, so I jog along at an even gait, my backpack swinging from side to side. I slow down as I get closer. There are dozens of people going in, so I won't be the last.

Five girls stand outside the gates. Five mops of black emo hair.

And in front of them is the girl with the purple streak.

FIVE

TAYLOR

THEY SPREAD OUT, TAKING up as much space as possible, forming a wall of flesh and bone, a human barrier to the school. They haven't clocked me yet. I suppose that's because I'm wearing the same uniform as everyone else. I keep my head down and, grip the straps of my backpack. I can hear the blood rushing in my ears.

I have to get past them. I need to get to class. The bell's going to ring any minute. But I can't do it. These girls aren't going anywhere. I'm not walking into an ambush.

My phone jingles as I duck behind a car. It's Lucy:

'Where are you? You can't be late again. Mrs Patel is spewing lava.'

I consider the possibilities. I'm a pretty good runner. Should I just go for it? Sprint past them into the school? My ankle still hurts but it would be worth it. They can't get me once I'm in there. They won't get past reception. They're not in uniform. And our receptionist is a dragon.

But what if I don't make it? There's so many of them. They could grab me, take me down. I rack my brains, trying to work out if I can get in round the side, somehow, or round the back. But they don't open those gates in the morning. There's no other way in. I could wait a few minutes and see if they leave? But then the gates will be locked and I'll have to go through reception and I'll be in trouble.

I stay down behind the car, watching as one of them lights a cigarette. Smoking is not allowed outside the school gates. There's a big sign and everything. I wait for one of the teachers to come out and confront them but no one does.

Another kid comes flying down the road. The girls let him pass. This just confirms it for me. They're not harassing everyone.

They're waiting for me.

It starts to rain. Big wet drops that slide down my sweaty face. Maybe this is just what I need to get rid of this lot. I check my phone. I still hear Lucy breathing on the other end.

'They're out here,' I whisper. 'Those girls.'

'What are you going to do?'

The girl who is smoking looks annoyed as her flame flickers in the rain. She stubs it out and casts her eye up and down the road. More late-comers appear like dots on the horizon. Some of them don't even pick up speed. They don't care about being late, perhaps they don't even notice. Not even the wind and the rain can make them go any faster. They just plod along like they have all the time in the world.

The girl with the purple streak sits down on the pavement. Despite the weather, she is wearing shorts, with her socks rolled up to her knees, her long hair in plaits either side of her head. I wonder why she's not in school. Why none of them are in school.

Perhaps they homeschool? The thought sends a shiver down my neck. If so, then no one will care that they're not in class. And they won't be in a rush to go anywhere. They can wait here all day if they choose. Is that what they're going to do?

One minute to go.

A car pulls up. A dozen kids spill out, some big, some small. I recognise the Battersea family. Their mum's still in her pyjamas, yelling instructions and tossing out backpacks and lunches. They all stop to hug her before they bundle towards the gates.

This is my chance, I realise. I could go in with them. And if the girls start on me, the biggest Batterseas are quite tough. They might help me out.

But even as I try to get up the nerve, it's already too late. The moment has passed. The Batterseas surge towards the door. Seconds later, they're inside.

Most of the cars have driven off now. There's only a couple left, including the one I'm hiding behind. I sink lower, feeling exposed. The street has become silent. The biggest girl steps away from the others, pacing left and right.

The bell sounds. If I'm going in, I've got to go now. My heart thumps. I don't know what to do. Then I notice a parent exiting the school gates. She's dressed in a smart suit and cloppy heels. She strides past the girls and starts to cross the road. She's returning to her car, I realise. The very one I'm hiding behind.

The car in front drives off, and there is nowhere for me to go. The woman glances questioningly at me as she gets into her car, and I wonder if I should say something. She starts the engine.

My cue to run.

I spring to my feet and immediately, cramp seizes my bad ankle. I pump my arms, forcing my legs to carry me along. I run back down the road and don't look back. I gasp for air as I hobble towards the tube station. I could get lucky. There might be a train waiting on the platform. But what if there isn't? I get a vision of them chasing me down, and shoving me onto the tracks.

No!

I keep going, round the corner and into a side road.

My ankle is throbbing and I have no idea what I'm doing. I spot a big yellow skip in somebody's garden and I run over and duck behind it. I don't know for sure if the girls are chasing me until I hear them coming, yelling to one another.

'Where did she go?'

My heart pounds. They must have seen me turn into this road. They know I'm here. Any minute they're going to find me. And then...

I close my eyes and wait. The minutes drag by and it occurs to me that I'm now horribly late for school. I check my phone. I should be in registration. When the register goes back to the office, my absence will trigger a phone call from the receptionist to my mum, and then I'll really be in the shit.

I risk a glance up and down the street. I can't see them. I google the school office and call.

'Hi. This is Taylor Applewood. I'm running late,' I whisper to the receptionist.

She sounds outraged. 'You need to get yourself to school. You're going to get a late mark.'

'Yes, I know. I'm sorry. I... ran into some trouble on the way.'

She doesn't ask me what sort of trouble. She doesn't give a rat's arse.

'I'm coming as soon as I can,' I say and hang up.

I breathe out. At least no one's going to call Mum and scare the crap out of her.

Still, I wait. It feels weird crouching behind somebody's skip. But I don't have any other option. There are six of them and only one of me. What else am I going to do?

After a while, I come out of my hiding place and look up and down the street. When I don't see anyone, I walk back towards the school. But as I reach the corner, I stop dead.

They are waiting for me, just outside the tube station.

What the hell am I going to do?

SIX

JOY

RIVERWOOD BUZZES WITH ACTIVITY. Shoppers weave through the crowd, arms laden with bags, while the faint strains of carols play overhead. A towering Christmas tree dominates the food court, its branches sagging under glittering baubles and oversized candy canes. I pull my scarf tighter, scanning the busy concourse, then I approach the Customer Services desk.

'Hi, I have a question for the security team,' I say.

The young chap nods at the adjacent desk. A woman in a high-vis vest sits behind a desk, her fingers tapping briskly at the keyboard. Standing beside her is a man with his arms crossed, his gaze fixed on the escalators as if anticipating trouble.

The man flicks a glance at me before resuming his watch. The woman stops typing.

'Can I help?'

I swallow the dryness in my throat. 'I was wondering if you were here yesterday? My daughter and her friend were here around four in the afternoon and a group of teenage girls chased them through the town. I'm trying to find out who they were.'

The man doesn't take his eye off the escalators. 'Teenagers,' he says, in the same tone you might use to say 'cockroaches.'

His female colleague cuts him a look that silences him immediately, then turns her attention back to me. 'Do you know which door they went out?'

'I'm not sure. Probably the one nearest the bus station.'

She nods. 'Let me see what I can find.'

She refocuses on the computer. Her fingers move so swiftly I can't see what she's doing.

I shift my weight slightly, my eyes drifting to the man. His posture is rigid, his gaze fixed on the shoppers using the escalators. I wonder if he can tell, just by watching their movements and body language, who's likely to cause trouble.

The woman turns her screen towards me.

'Can you see them?'

I step closer, my pulse quickening as the footage plays.

'That's my daughter,' I say, watching as Taylor and Lucy emerge from Pemberley's. They haven't noticed yet, but the girls are already closing in on them. There are two groups of them. One comes from the top floor, where the restaurants are, and the other waits on the floor below. I watch as they all converge on the escalators. Taylor and Lucy look as though they are chatting away, totally oblivious as the girl gang closes in on them like sharks.

The security guard zooms in a little. The smallest girl looks like a skunk with that weird mauve streak in her hair. The older ones look like they're off to a rock concert. I'm guessing they're fans of My Chemical Romance, or whatever they listen to now. Every last one of them has the same black wavy hair and pale skin.

They move as a unit, their heads tilted close together, their movements unnervingly deliberate. There's a calculated confidence about them that sets my stomach on edge, as if they already know they can't be stopped.

The security guard zooms in closer and I study their faces, trying to commit every detail to memory. Why did they follow Taylor and Lucy? My first thought is that they were planning to mug them, but they are too open about it. There is no obvious attempt to cover up what they're doing. Pure hooliganism then.

'Can I get a copy of this?' I ask.

She shakes her head. 'Sorry, we can't release footage without an official request. Data protection laws.'

I tap my fingers against the counter. 'Can you show it to the police?'

'If they request it, we'll provide it.'

I nod. At least I know what they look like now. And I've seen what happened. It looks as though Taylor was telling the truth.

'Thank you,' I say, stepping back.

As I turn to leave, the other security guard looks at me properly for the first time.

'Has anyone ever told you you're the spitting image of Joy Applewood. The rallycross driver?'

I force a smile. 'Yeah, I've heard that before.'

His gaze lingers on me for a second too long before he turns back to the escalators. The woman, engrossed in the security footage, doesn't look up.

I walk back out to the car park, my eyes scanning for any sign of the gang. They should be in school at this time of day, but I wouldn't be surprised to find them hanging around out here. As I pass a couple of men smoking joints, the sweet but heady smell hits me, and I hold my breath, quickening my pace.

The place is a mess. Broken glass is scattered across the pavement, and an upturned trolley lies abandoned in the middle of the road, wheels spinning in the breeze. It's hard to believe the shopping centre was only built five years ago. I still think of it as new, but looking around now, it's clear the shine has worn off.

There was a stabbing in the park just a couple of months ago. It's hard not to think about it every time I walk past. And only last week, a pensioner was shoved under a bus. That one made the national news. My friend Aimee has been banging on about how bad things are getting for months. I suppose I should've listened because she's right—this whole area is going downhill.

Back in the car, I think over what I've discovered. Those girls aren't just dangerous, they're calculated, predatory. But if they even think about coming near Taylor again, they've got another thing c   o   m   -ing.

SEVEN

TAYLOR

I LOOK ACROSS THE road at the girls. They spread out in front of the tube station, taking up half the pavement like they own the place.

My stomach tightens. There's nothing for it. I have to run. Before I can think twice, I'm flying along, legs pumping as I sprint full pelt towards the school.

My heart pounds in my ears. I don't know how much longer I can run like this. I glance back. Relief floods my veins as I realise they haven't even seen me. The middle one finishes her vape, then they disappear inside.

I slow to a walk, gasping to get my breath back. My heart is still thumping as I reach the school and I'm pretty certain my face is bright red. I go to open the gate, but then I see the padlock.

Damn.

I walk through the staff car park, and up the ramp to reception.

I press the button and stand outside, puffing and panting as I wait to be let in. I pull out my water bottle, take a long gulp, and wipe my mouth with the back of my hand.

The receptionist buzzes me in.

I'm twenty-five minutes late.

Fantastic.

The receptionist glares at me, her face colder than the weather outside.

'Sign the late book,' she snaps, sliding the pen toward me like it's a chore just to deal with me.

My hand shakes as I pick it up, and the letters I scribble barely look like my name. The pen slips once, leaving an awkward streak on the page.

She stares at me like I'm some kind of freak.

'Right,' she says, her voice clipped. 'You better get to class. And if you're late again, it's going on your *permanent record*.'

Permanent record? Seriously? But I keep my head down, mumble something that might pass for "sorry," and get out of there as fast as I can.

I get a sugar rush the minute I enter the Home Economics room. The rest of the class are already stationed at their little kitchenette islands, hard at work. The teacher, Miss Matthews, stands at the front of the room, her apron speckled with flour.

She gives me a tight smile.

'If you work quickly, you should be able to catch up.'

I scan the room. The only free workstation seat is next to Star. She already has her ingredients spread out neatly in front of her.

'Where have you been?' she asks in a hushed tone.

I ignore her and slump down in my seat. My hands are shaking and I think I might be sick.

'We're making souffle.' Star says. 'Hurry up. We've got to get them in the oven.'

I haul myself to my feet and stagger over to the counter. I pick up the sugar and attempt to pour it into a measuring bowl but half of it ends up on my shoes. I feel Star's eyes on me. Miss Mathews' too.

I look up at the board to check out the rest of the measurements, but my head is swimming.

I see those girls. The mean smiles. The hungry eyes. They all have that same look, and I'm starting to get a really bad feeling about them.

I think I might know who they are.

I tap my smartwatch and type in the name 'Callaghan.'

There are hundreds of hits. I narrow it down to my area, and there they are, the six of them in a photo taken by the local paper a few weeks ago: they are all squeezed onto one sofa, with their miserable looking mum in the middle.

'Taylor!'

I jump right out of my skin as Miss Mathews looms over me. I crack the egg whites into a bowl and start to whisk. My hand starts aching immediately. They are supposed to turn into neat white peaks but it's not happening. And now my butter mixture is burning on the stove. I take it off the heat and pour it all into ramekins, then whack them into the oven.

I want to go home. I want to crawl into my bed and stay there.

Star is at the sink, washing up the bowls. I go to the window and watch in case they come back.

The timer goes off, making me jump. I rush over to the oven.

'Oven gloves!' Star shrieks, as I peer inside.

But what good are oven gloves when you already know you're going to get burnt?

It's no surprise when my souffles come out flat and deflated. Of course, Star's are totally lit. I feel a twinge of irritation as Miss Mathews drags Mr Chikondi in from the next room to admire them. I'm getting stomach cramps. I don't know if it's my period coming a week early, or just my body's response to all the stress I'm under.

Miss Mathews is talking to me, offering me advice on what I should do the next time, as if I'll ever make souffles again.

'Is everything alright?' she asks, when I don't respond.

'Yeah, fine.'

She gives me a long, lingering look, like she doesn't believe me and I force my mouth into a smile. I wish everyone would just piss off so I can hear myself think.

At home time, I'm allowed out early to collect my souffles. As I head towards Home Ec, I notice the door to the tech room is open. I peer inside and see the room is empty. The walls are covered with equipment: rulers, screwdrivers and drills. I slip inside, and pick up one of the electric drills. Then I put it down and pick up a hammer, feeling the weight of it in my hands.

I slip it into my bag.

'Taylor?'

I turn and see Mr Chikondi walk into the room.

I feel my cheeks burn red and I fumble for something to say.

'Can I help you?' he asks.

I look at his kind brown eyes and wonder if I should say something. Maybe he could help me. He could check to make sure they're not out there. Or he could let me hide in his classroom until they've gone.

But what if he rang the police?

My stomach shrivels at the thought.

'Dungeons and Dragons,' I say with desperation.

His eyes widen. 'You want to join the club?'

'Thought I might...give it a go.'

He twiddles his bowtie and looks ridiculously happy. It's just a lunchtime club. A really lame one at that. It's all nerds and kids who like drawing on their arms. Everyone makes fun of them. But I can't care about that right now, if it gets me off the hook.

'Well there's only one more session before Christmas,' he says. 'But you are more than welcome to join. We meet here at twelve thirty every Friday.'

'Y...yes.'

'Wonderful, I'll see you then.'

I exhale and slip into the Home Ec room where the rest of the class are collecting their Tupperware boxes with the souffles in them. Mine are such a mess I would dump them straight in the bin, if it weren't for the fact that this gets me out early.

I go to the window. I can't see any sign of those girls. They're not where they were this morning. I can see the bus waiting outside the gates though. My house is walking distance but this might be the safer option.

I try to keep with my class as they stream across the playground. I watch as Miss Dunstanburgh opens the gates with a creak.

My eyes flit from left to right, my heart thumping as I pass her. The bus is right in front of me. I just have to get from the gates to the bus, but if they are there, they might follow me. It's obvious they don't go to our school, but is anyone really going to stop them if they get on and beat me up?

I stand close to Kade Savage, a big brick of a Year Ten. He's all shoulders, with a face like a bulldog.

There is a lull as everyone has to swipe their bus pass. I jiggle about impatiently, eager to get on. Kade shoves his way through and I'm stuck behind a pair of Year Seven girls.

C'mon....

I can see a group of people walking up the road. From this distance, I can't tell if it's the Callaghans, but the mere thought sends me into a tizzy. I can't take it any more, I push my way past the younger girls and head for the top deck.

I sit behind Kade in the middle of the bus, holding my souffles. I keep an eye out for the girls but I can't see them. A bunch of Year Twos get on behind me. There is a rumble as the bus finally gets going.

'Let's see what you made then,' a boy from the class below is looking over my shoulder, trying to get.

'They're souffles,' I say with a yawn.

'Give us one.'

'They didn't turn out right.'

He pulls a face. 'You just want them all for yourself.'

I point over at Star, who's sitting three seats in front of me. 'Star's came out well. Ask her.'

I feel a twinge of satisfaction as the boy goes and bothers my former friend. Take that, Star.

It's a short journey and soon the bus pulls up at the stop across the road from my house. I clamber out quickly and bolt inside.

I burst inside and dump the souffles on the kitchen counter. Dad is already home. I let him make me a cup of tea. He likes to hear about my day. I try to come up with an interesting anecdote, but all I can think of is my deflated souffle.

A little later, Mum comes home with Clara. Clara is wearing her ridiculous costume again. I pretend not to notice as she rushes up to her room to change. I'll be glad when this nativity is over. Mum smiles at me.

'How was your day?'

'Fine.'

I stick a couple of crumpets in the toaster and go through the cupboards, looking for something else to eat. 'You'll spoil your dinner,' Mum says.

'What is it?'

'Chicken curry.'

'I don't like chicken curry.'

Mum looks injured. 'I thought you did?'

'No, that's Clara.'

'Oh.'

I'm messing with her. We both like it.

I close the cupboard door and glance out at the street.

My heart nearly stops.

They're out there. At the bus stop across the road. And they're looking right at my house.

EIGHT
TAYLOR

I YANK THE BLINDS shut. I feel as though I've just swallowed broken glass.

I grip the edge of the windowsill and my legs tremble beneath me.

But I can't help myself. I peek through a gap in the slats.

'Mum, they're out there!' I hiss.

I turn, but Mum's already left the room. I drop to the floor and crawl out of the kitchen on my hands and knees. I crouch in the hallway. My lungs are glitching and I'm hiccupping like a frog in a Coke can.

What do I do?

I hurry up the stairs and into my bedroom. I rush to the window and take another look. They're still there. The youngest one sits cross-legged on the pavement. The oldest is scrolling through her phone. And the others? They just stand there.

Watching.

Waiting.

I reach for my phone.

> *Those girls are outside my house.*

Lucy replies almost immediately:

> *Have you told your parents?*

I hesitate. The idea of Mum storming out there, all righteous fury, fills me with dread.

> *No. I don't want to worry them.*

I think you should. This is getting crazy.

Crazy doesn't even begin to cover it. I glance out the window again. The pale glow of the streetlights makes their faces look ghostly. Some of them aren't even wearing coats. How can they stand the cold? My teeth chatter just looking at them.

I drop the curtain and sit cross-legged on my bed, trying to focus on a game on my phone. Bright colours flash across the screen, but I'm not really seeing them. I force myself to keep playing until I've completed three rounds. Then I take another look.

Still out there. The youngest traces patterns in the dirt. The rest just stand perfectly still, like statues. They're doing it on purpose. They're trying to freak me out. I never thought you could be stalked by a group of people, but it seems you can.

I sit at my computer and log on to the maths app. Ugh, algebra. I watch the video, explaining what I have to do for my homework, but I can't take it in. The numbers all blur together.

Whatever they are going to do, I wish they'd just do it. It's the waiting I can't stand.

My stomach rumbles. I never did eat my after-school snack. I plod downstairs to the kitchen. The blinds are still drawn so they won't know I'm in here. I switch on the kettle. The crumpets I made earlier are like soggy coasters. I throw them in the bin and toast some fresh ones and rummage through the fridge for the spread.

When my food's ready, I carry it into the living room, where I find Clara sprawled on the sofa, glued to the TV. When the credits roll, I change the channel. For once, she doesn't whine. I grab one of her dolls, the one with tangled pink hair, and start plaiting. The repetitive motion steadies my nerves, my fingers twisting and weaving the frizzy strands.

I make up my mind that if the Callaghans are still out there at dinner time, I'll tell Mum and Dad.

When Dad calls us for dinner, I hesitate. My legs feel heavy as I walk to the window, tugging the blinds aside just enough to peek out. My breath catches.

The street is empty. I scan up and down, my heart hammering, but there's no sign of them.

Finally.

I let out a shaky breath and pull the blinds open properly. The evening light streams in, and the tension in my chest loosens. My shoulders slump as I shuffle to the table and drop into my chair. My legs judder like I've just crossed a finish line.

Dinner passes in a blur. Clara chatters endlessly about her show, while Mum and Dad beam like she's the next West End star. I shovel food into my mouth without tasting it, nodding in the right places, but all the while, I'm watching the road outside.

Watching for them.

Afterwards, Clara and I clear the table. Plates clink against each other as I load them into the dishwasher. Could they still be out there? The sun has set by now, and it's hard to see past my own reflection. I look out at a sea of darkness. The streetlights are lighthouses, warning traffic with their halos of light. Busses and cars drift past like ghost ships, their headlights slicing through the gloom.

Are they still out there?

I feed the dishwasher a tablet and switch it on. It clears its throat, then the rumbling starts, swishing and gargling, like Dad does when he uses mouthwash.

I go to the door and open it cautiously, stepping out onto the porch. My breath puffs out in little thin clouds. The street is silent, empty. Relief washes over me, but it's fleeting.

They know where I live now.

They can come back anytime.

Inside, I lock the door and lean against it, my heart battering against my ribs.

What do I do?

What the hell do I do?

I'm up four or five times in the night. Each time I sit up and check to make sure they're gone. The shadows shift and ripple in the wind, twisting into shapes that mess with my head.

I wake up insanely early, feeling like a zombie. My eyes are gritty and my head feels like it weighs a ton. The first thing I do is check to see if they're out there. There's no sign of them. I'm almost disappointed.

At least then I'd know where they are.

I decide to go to school early. Our school has a free breakfast club, you just pay a donation and you get cereal and toast. Plus, they let you use the computers, so I could finish the maths.

Mum and Dad are still in their dressing gowns as I leave the house. Dad raises an eyebrow.

'You're keen!'

I force a smile, but it drops the second I set foot outside. My steps become heavier as I leave our street. The road's practically empty, and every corner feels like a trap. What if the girls are waiting somewhere? They could jump me, and no one would even be around to stop them.

I slow down even more, my stomach twisting, but I don't see them. Just a homeless woman curled up in a sleeping bag on the pavement. She's out cold, oblivious. Must be nice.

I watch the entrance to the tube station. A crowd of people pours out, but the girls are not there. I dart past, breaking into a jog. I can see the school. I just have to get there in one piece.

The car park's already packed. Guess the teachers have to be in early to get everything sorted. I keep my head down and walk fast, aiming straight for the breakfast club, when I hear footsteps behind me.

'Taylor?'

I whip round. Then I see it's just Miss Todd, one of the teaching assistants. I let out a shaky breath and force myself to relax, trying to act like I wasn't just about to bolt.

She gives me a small, friendly smile. 'Taylor, have you thought about joining the rugby team? We could really use someone like you.'

'Rugby?' I shake my head. 'I'm more of a cricket person.'

'I know,' she says, tilting her head, 'but it's good to stay fit in the off-season. Rugby would be perfect for that.'

Out of the corner of my eye, I catch sight of the girls walking up the road from the tube. Their eyes lock in on me like predators spotting prey. But they won't do anything if I'm with a teacher. Right? They wouldn't dare. My stomach twists into a knot and I slip my hand into my bag, my fingers closing around the hammer.

'Would you help me carry some boxes inside?' Miss Todd asks, oblivious to the storm building inside me.

I nod automatically because what else can I do? My stomach churns and my hands shake so badly I almost drop my bag.

I glance back. The girls are speeding up, hurrying along the road towards me as Miss Todd pops open her boot. She's smiling as she unloads junk into my arms—boxes of balls and beanbags, hula hoops, and even traffic cones.

'They were giving all this away at the sports centre. Can you believe it?' she says brightly.

I can't answer. My throat feels like it's closing up, and my heart is racing too fast for me to think straight. I glance back again. They're outside now, crossing the car park towards me.

'Miss Todd,' I manage to croak.

She doesn't notice. She's still fiddling with something in the boot. My legs scream at me to move, to run, but my arms are loaded. I walk ahead of her, up the ramp to reception. I shoulder the door, but it's locked.

I turn and look at Miss Todd. It's like that feeling you get when you're a little kid and you really have to pee.

C'mon...

She finally shuts the boot and carries a big box of stuff over to me, then stands there fiddling with her lanyard. I hold my breath as I wait for her to swipe us in. The door creaks open. I wait for Miss Todd to go inside, then I rush in after her, the pile of junk teetering in my arms. Miss Todd walks ahead, heading towards the sports hall. I dump everything onto the floor and dart back to the door. It's one of those automatic ones and it's closing at a painfully slow rate, inch by inch, just as the Callaghans are coming up the ramp. One of them lunges for it but I push it shut. The heavy click of the lock echoes in the small space and the glass rattles.

I start to hiccup. Through the glass, I see their faces, twisted with hate. One of them slams her palm against the door. The sound makes me flinch. Are they going to break the door down? I don't wait to see. I gather up all the stuff I dropped and hurry after Miss Todd.

I find her in the storeroom, and I unload everything onto the floor.

She beams at me. 'Thank you so much for your help! I take it you're off to the breakfast club?'

'Yes.'

I realise with a jolt that I have to go back outside to reach it. The entrance is on the other side of the car park.

'Would you like some help to put all this stuff away?' I ask hopefully.

'Oh no, that's fine, thank you. I'm not sure where it's going to go yet.'

She gives a careless chuckle and I force a smile. 'Okay, see you later. Hic!'

'Bye Taylor. Thanks again.'

I take a couple of steps towards the door.

There's no way I'm going out there. I'll have to hide in the hall, or perhaps in the staff toilets. I'm not really allowed, but what choice do I have?

'You can cut through the hall,' she says, as if reading my mind. 'It's the red door on the right of Mrs Claxon's office.'

I could hug her.

'Thank you.'

But first I head back to reception. I watch as the girls press their noses against the glass like a pack of hungry dogs. What's their game plan? Are they just going to stand there and wait to be let in?

I dart back the other way, through the hall like Miss Todd suggested, and into the breakfast club. I sit at one of the computers and start my maths homework, but I keep my bag on my lap the whole time, and one eye on the door.

NINE
JOY

HOWARD MOVES ABOUT THE kitchen with a quiet efficiency, unpacking the shopping. He stacks the tins neatly in the cupboard, then opens the egg box to check none of them have cracked in transit. The last item, a jar of pasta sauce slips from his hand and he catches it mid-air. He looks across the room at me and grins like he's just won the Grand Prix. I smile back and go out to the living room to see what the kids are up to.

Clara sprawls on the floor, surrounded by her dolls. She chatters to them nonstop, creating elaborate storylines involving multiple manipulations and betrayals. I blame it on the soaps Taylor watches.

'No, Princess Emily! You can't marry him!' she says, holding up one doll dramatically. 'He's a bad man in disguise! He wants to put you to sleep and steal all your horses!'

My heart floods with love. Clara's hair is a mess of wild curls, her cheeks flushed with the excitement of her imaginary drama.

She's always been like this—so full of life it spills out of her, infecting everything around her.

I hear footsteps thudding down the stairs, heavy and deliberate.

'Mum, can we order pizza tonight?' Taylor asks as she stalks into the room.

She's tied her lovely blonde hair back in a severe bun that makes her look like a drill sergeant. Just a couple of years ago, her wardrobe was all rainbow leggings and sequined tops. Now she practically lives in the same old baggy grey hoodie she always wears, her hands stuffed into its kangaroo pocket.

'We're having lasagna,' I say firmly.

She rolls her eyes. 'Great. More burnt food.'

'It won't be burnt,' I assure her, although Howard's signature dish is admittedly a bit hit-or-miss.

Taylor plops onto the sofa, her dark mood settling over us all like a cloud.

'You're sitting on Mr Whiskers,' Clara says, pointing to the plastic cat trapped under Taylor's leg.

Taylor leans back against the sofa. 'Oh no. Should we call an ambulance?'

I look over at her. 'Give him back to your sister.'

Taylor sighs dramatically, shifting just enough to dislodge the toy. 'There. Happy now?'

Clara picks up the little cat, brushing it off like it's been genuinely harmed. 'You squished him.'

Taylor snorts. 'It's a lump of plastic, Clara. Get a grip. It's not real, you know.'

Clara hugs the cat protectively, her cheeks reddening. 'You don't have to be so mean.'

Taylor smirks. 'Mean? Seriously? You're almost nine, and you still play with dolls. It's embarrassing. No wonder you don't have any friends.'

Clara stiffens and her jaw tightens.

'Taylor,' I say sharply.

It isn't even true. Clara has plenty of friends. Taylor, on the other hand...

Taylor glances at me with a raised eyebrow, then shrugs like she's done nothing wrong.

'Whatever,' she says. She jumps down off the sofa, deliberately walking through the dolls as she heads for the door. I open my mouth to call her back, then I change my mind. She doesn't listen to a word I say these days. If I tell her off, she's just as likely to give me lip. It's like she doesn't care what I think of her anymore.

I look down at Clara, who goes back to her game. They've always bickered. What sisters don't? But it's more than that. Taylor is different. I feel it in the way she avoids my eyes. She's locking us out of her world.

I miss her.

The old Taylor. The one who would have sat on the floor with Clara and made up a ridiculous story about Mr Whiskers. The one who used to sit on the counter while I cooked, telling me the latest gossip from school.

I don't know where she's gone.

Sunday morning, I have a long lie in because there's really no reason to get up. It feels good because I've been dog tired all week. I wake naturally and wander downstairs to the kitchen where Howard is frying bacon for brunch.

Clara comes in and crawls under the table with her dolls.

'What are you doing?' I ask.

'We're in the bunker.'

'Why?'

'There's a war going on.'

I almost forget she's there as I help slice bread for toast and set the table.

'Shall I go and get Taylor?' I ask, when the food is ready.

Howard thinks it over. 'Nah, let her sleep.'

I think what he means is that it will be nice to have a peaceful meal without Taylor winding Clara up.

The three of us sit at the table, Clara sneaking bites to Emily while we eat. She's not supposed to have her dolls at the table, but I can see her on her lap. Once again, I turn a blind eye.

'How are the rehearsals going?' Howard asks, breaking the silence.

'Good,' Clara says.

I smile at her fondly. The first performance is on Wednesday and she can't wait. The drama teacher's coming from the Academy to watch and you'd think she was a talent scout, coming to sign them all up for Hollywood.

'I see you haven't left anything for me,' Taylor says, making me jump.

I look up to see her standing in the doorway, still dressed in that awful grey hoodie. She has bags under her eyes despite her lie in.

'We thought we should let you sleep,' Howard says. 'Why don't you take a seat, and I'll fry you up some fresh bacon?'

Taylor flumps down and Clara jumps up from the table.

'Right, I'm going out to play.'

Taylor jerks her head up. 'No, you can't!'

We all look at her.

'Why ever not?' I ask.

Taylor looks at me directly. She speaks so quietly, I can barely hear her.

'Those girls are out there. The ones from Riverwood.'

We all turn and look out of the window.

Six girls stare back.

TEN
JOY

THE GANG STAND AS still as statues. I get a good look at them. They're all dark-haired and pale skinned. Definitely sisters, or maybe cousins. They stand in a similar way and have the same spiteful eyes. I'm in no doubt that these are the girls I saw on the CCTV the other day.

'What are they? Zombies?' Howard says, standing behind me.

'Well, they don't scare me,' Clara says, heading towards the door.

'Clara, wait!' I grab her hand and pull her back.

'What? They're just standing there.'

'I know, but...'

I look at Howard, who gives me a helpless shrug. Fury warms my chest. I feel it radiating through my limbs. This is my house, my family. They have no right to intimidate us like this.

'Mum, what are you doing?' Taylor's voice cracks as I shove my feet into my shoes.

Even Howard looks uneasy, his brow furrowed.

'I'm going to have a word.'

I smooth out my jumper and take a deep breath, letting my face settle into a neutral expression—not hostile, but far from friendly.

Howard steps closer. 'Joy...'

I meet his eye. 'I'll be fine.'

I open the door and step out onto the porch. The cold air bites my cheeks, but I barely feel it. The girls' heads tilt towards me in the exact same gesture. It's uncanny.

My steps falter.

'Can I help you?' I say, arms crossed.

They stare through me like I'm not even there.

I take a step towards them and then, splat! Something hard and wet hits me square in the forehead, and a thick, sticky liquid drips down my temple. Shock freezes me in place. I reach up and find my hand covered in egg yolk. There are bits of shell on the pavement and on my shoe.

Before I can react, another egg hits my shoulder. The girl's pockets are stuffed with them. They throw one after another. I spin round, and more eggs explode against my back. The pavement around me looks like a battleground, yolk and shells splattering like tiny bombs. As I race back into the house, I hear their laughter echoing down the street. I imagine the neighbours' curtains twitching as they peer through their windows. I hope they have seen this, because the more witnesses,say, the better.

Howard pulls me inside, slamming the door shut behind me.

'Joy, are you okay?' His hands hover over me, unsure where to start.

Clara runs up and hugs me, and I let her even knowing she'll get covered in egg as well.

Taylor gives me a sour look and turns her back on me. 'I told you not to go out there, Mum.'

'I'm fine,' I say, wiping my face with a tea towel.

I shudder as a yolk slides down my neck.

'They're still out there,' I say nodding at the window.

'Good. Call the police.'

I shower quickly. The hot water scalds my skin, but I don't care. I wash away the egg and the humiliation, then change into a clean set of clothes.

'Are you sure you're alright?' Howard asks when I get back downstairs. He pulls me to him and brushes a kiss across my damp hair.

I nod. 'What did the police say?'

He pulls a face. 'They might come round later.'

'Might?' I frown. 'It's anti-social behaviour, isn't it?'

He nods. 'We need to document it. Keep a record.'

'Should we film them?'

'I don't know if we're allowed.'

We head out to the lounge, where Taylor sits glued to her phone and Clara plays with her dolls in front of the TV. Taylor looks very sullen, I think and I wonder if she's feeling scared. After all, this all started with her.

After a few minutes, she gets up and leaves the room.

Howard shoots me a look. 'Should I go and talk to her?'

I'm about to answer when she comes running back in.

'Mum! Dad! They've crossed the street. They're outside our house!'

ELEVEN

JOY

HOWARD CALLS THE POLICE again while I rush around the house, checking the locks and closing all the curtains and blinds so they can't see in. My pulse races as I spot them just outside the kitchen window. They're deliberately trampling the flower beds, grinding their shoes into the soil.

I turn and see Howard behind me. 'What did the police say?'

'They're on their way.'

I feel a rush of relief. 'But what are we meant to do in the meantime?'

I jump as one of them raps on the window, and then the others are at it. They're on all sides of the house. Knocking and banging on the doors and windows. It feels like we are under attack.

Howard straightens up. 'Maybe I should have a word with them?'

I blink. Confrontation isn't his forte. Usually, that's my role.

'I really don't think...'

He looks at me. 'They're just a bunch of girls, aren't they?' He glances back at Taylor, who is hovering about like a shadow. 'You stay with Clara.'

My heart is in my mouth as he goes to the side door. I never knew he had it in him. He unlocks it quickly, and I lean against it, to make sure they don't get in. I watch as he walks up to one of the older ones.

'Hello,' he says in his calm, measured way.

I can't hear the rest of what he says, but I see his hands gesturing, his palms up in a placating manner. The girls stare back at him, their expressions unchanged. His voice rises a little and I catch the words 'dignified' and 'respect.'

Oh god, he sounds like a school teacher.

Now he's walking back towards the door. I open it quickly. The youngest girl appears out of nowhere and barrels her way in. Taylor grabs her and tosses her out like the cat at the end of the Flintstones. I lock the door and move everyone away in case they manage to break the glass. My heart is pounding like crazy.

Where the hell are the police?

I turn and look at Howard.

'What did they say?' I ask.

He looks down at his feet.

'They said, "It's not your fight, old man".'

'You're so embarrassing!' Taylor says, shaking her head.

I turn on her. 'That's enough out of you. Your dad was just trying to sort out your mess.'

Taylor's mouth falls open, and I immediately regret my words. I didn't really mean that. It's not her fault these girls are being so awful. I just want them to stop making all that racket. I can't hear myself think.

I go and check on Clara, but she doesn't seem the least bit scared. Her dolls are having a party. They've got biscuits on plates—a whole pack of Jammie Dodgers. She must have swiped them from the kitchen.

'Can you play with me?' she asks.

'Not right now,' I say, covering my ears.

How long are they going to stay out there?

I think about our next-door neighbour, Laszlo. He usually keeps himself to himself, but he's ex-army, so he might be handy in this situation. Unfortunately, I don't have his number. I mention him to Howard, and we debate whether one of us should run next door to get him.

'I'll go,' I say. 'You went out last.'

'No, I think it should be me,' Howard says.

'The police are coming!' Taylor yells from the window.

Clara jumps to her feet. 'I want to see the police!'

'Clara, this is serious business,' I say.

I go to the window and watch as the car pulls up outside our house.

I look for the girls, but there's no sign of them. How is that possible? They were here just a minute ago.

I dash to the door, but it's as if they've just melted away into thin air. I look up and down the street, wondering if they've ducked into someone's garden. I run round the back and check they're not hiding in ours, but there's no one out there except next door's tomcat, Muppet.

Howard lets the police in, and I make them a cup of tea. It's the least I can do. There's a young Asian woman and a man who seems much older, although he's prematurely balding. They're very nice. I'm not sure if they're real police or Community Support Officers. I can't tell the difference these days.

They go through the procedures for dealing with antisocial behaviour, and I listen as Taylor recounts how all this started. Her voice is small, her hands twisting in her lap.

'They've been hanging around outside my school,' she admits.

'Why didn't you say?' I ask.

'I was embarrassed,' she says, not looking at me. 'They stood outside my school yesterday Thursday and Friday morning, waiting for me.'

'That's harassment,' Howard says, looking at the police for confirmation.

The policeman is writing it all down in his little book. What neat handwriting he has—very square and loopy. I bet he got good marks at school.

'So you need to keep a record. That's the best thing you can do,' the female officer advises.

'Have you any idea what their names are?'

We look at each other, but nobody says anything.

'I think they're related to each other,' I say. 'They've got a look about them—dark hair and pale skin. I think they're sisters. The security people at the Riverwood Centre caught them on camera, because it all started there. You can get the images from them.'

'Very good. And there are six of them, you say?'

'Yeah, all different ages.'

The two police officers look at each other as if trying to figure out if they know them.

'Doesn't ring a bell' the policeman says.

'No, I can't say it does, but we'll certainly keep an eye out. Do you know if they've bothered any of the neighbours?'

'Not that we know of.'

'We can try having a word with them, see if they've seen anything.'

'So what am I supposed to do?' Taylor asks. 'If they turn up at school again?'

'Tell a teacher.'

'But I can't get into school if they stand outside.'

'I'll take you in,' Howard offers. 'Until all this blows over.'

Taylor looks taken aback. I see her weighing it up in her mind.

Howard smiles. 'What's wrong? You don't want people knowing you've got parents? Where do you think you came from—a gooseberry bush?'

Clara laughs like a hyena. But I understand Taylor's dilemma. She doesn't want to look like a baby.

'You could drop me at the breakfast club,' she concedes.

'If you prefer,' Howard says.

'Thank you for the tea,' the policewoman says, standing up. 'I'm sorry we couldn't be any immediate help. Like I said, make sure you keep a record of everything and let us know if there are any further incidents.'

She hands me a business card.

'Thank you,' I say, slipping it into my pocket.

Once the police have departed, Howard looks at Taylor. 'Are you absolutely sure nothing happened to spark this behaviour when you and Lucy were at the shopping centre?' he says.

'No, Dad, we didn't do anything. I swear.'

He nods. 'Then are they also stalking Lucy?'

'I don't think so.'

'They didn't bother her when they were outside the school?'

'She didn't even notice them.'

'And she hasn't seen anyone hanging around outside her house?'

'No.'

I don't miss the flicker of doubt in his eyes.

'So it's just us they've got a vendetta against?'

Taylor mutters something and stomps up to her room.

TWELVE

JOY

IT'S MY DAY TO work from home, and if I'm honest, I enjoy it when the house is all quiet. Much as I love my family, I live for these small pockets of calm. I should be sitting at my desk, but instead, I potter around the house, dealing with little tasks I'd never get done otherwise.

I've already cleaned the kitchen, and now I head upstairs to the children's rooms with a basket full of laundry. I hang up Clara's dresses, then step into Taylor's room. Opening her wardrobe, I hang up her jeans and t-shirts. When I've finished, I stay and tidy a little—picking up dirty underwear from the floor and tossing it into the laundry basket. I know she should do it herself, but I can't stand the mess.

Two dirty plates sit on her bedside table. I pick them up, along with a teacup, and place them by the door. Her desk, in contrast, is surprisingly tidy. A neat pile of notebooks catches my eye, and I pick one up. What neat handwriting she has these days. It's nice to see her taking pride in her work. I flip through the book, smiling as I read her take on various historical events. The writing loses its neatness towards the end of the book. There are ink splodges and lots of crossings out. It's hard to believe they were written by the same girl.

I spot a sweet wrapper sticking out of her desk drawer. I open it and find several more. I pull them out and toss them into the bin. At the very back of the drawer, I notice a smaller notebook. I pluck it out. The pink faux-leather cover is scuffed and peeling at the edges. I glance towards the door, then flip it open.

The first few pages are as I would expect, grumbles about school, complaints about Clara, snarky observations about her teachers. I can hear her voice in these first carefully written words. But about halfway through, the tone shifts completely. She goes days without writing, and when she resumes, the notes are more cryptic and difficult to decipher. She has switched to a red pen, and there are a lot of doodles and the odd scrawled sentence that I can't make out. I flip forward a few more pages. She's switched to a black pen and the words are legible again:

'Sold pills to Year 11s.'

My stomach drops. I flip to the next page.

'Thinking about dealing to the Year 7s. Easy targets, fewer questions.'

My chest tightens as I read the words again, my mind racing.
Oh, Taylor! What have you got yourself into?
The entries spiral from there. There is a series of dates and names:

'Mr T at number 14.
LW at the bus stop.
Get more Coke for Mrs Dunstanburgh.'

Her teacher?
I drop the book and pick it up from the floor. I stare at the words again, trying to make sense of them. She has to mean Cola, right? She's getting Mrs Dunstanburgh a drink.
I turn the page, and scrawled in large, angry letters it says:

'Fuck off, Mum.'

The words hit harder than any of her ridiculous confessions.
I close the diary for a moment, my hands shaking. She wrote this for me, didn't she? A booby trap, in case I dared to look.

My eyes sting, but I blink the tears away. I know I should never have looked, but I've been so worried.

I look through the diary again, scanning the pages with new eyes. Beneath these ridiculous entries, there's a thread of something real. There's a date midway through where the handwriting becomes more rushed and the tone more erratic. It's around that same time Taylor started to change. When she stopped talking to me, and started pulling away from everything she used to care about.

I hold the diary for a moment. The truth is buried in here, somewhere between the lies and the anger. I don't know how much of what I've just read is real, but one thing is clear:

I'm losing her.

THIRTEEN
JOY

FRIDAY NIGHT IS CLARA'S nativity. Actually, she's already performed it four times before we get to see it. She's given performances in assembly at school, and for other local schools. And then a matinee, for parents with young pre-school children. We choose to attend the evening performance where there's less chance of kids screaming. It's easier to fit around work, and besides, the last performance is always the best.

Clara is fully warmed up, confident of her part and she's high on the drama of it all.

'Make sure you sit right at the front,' she warns as we drop her off.

'We'll do our best,' Howard says, with an eye to the crowd of parents waiting to go in.

Fortunately we have Taylor, who worms her way through the crowd and manages to bag front row seats, allowing Howard and I to enter in a more polite and dignified manner.

Taylor sits there with her arms at her sides, like she's fulfilling military duty and when we reach the front row, she acknowledges us with a subtle nod of the head, just so as not to spoil the illusion that she's an orphan.

She stares at her phone as we wait for the play to start but as soon as the curtain comes up, she slides it back into her pocket and looks attentive as Clara takes to the stage and begins the show. Clara doesn't look remotely nervous. Where does that incredible confidence come from? I hope she never loses it.

It all goes well until about halfway through the performance. Mary and Joseph are nicely kitted out in the stables despite getting lost on the way, and the three wise men have done their Christmas shopping, picking up some wonderful bargains at their local supermarket.

'I mean, I like gold as much as the next person. But what's a baby going to do with frankincense?' Clara derides them. 'And what the hell is myrrh?'

Taking her advice, they instead purchase a teddy bear, nappies and a nice warm blanket and navigate the desert roads to arrive in Bethlehem, just in time for the birth of Jesus Christ.

At this point, Mary is given privacy to birth the baby while Clara entertains everyone with a beautiful solo. It is the most heartfelt song of the night, and the whole audience is on tenterhooks. She goes for it, screwing up her face in concentration as she hits the high C. All at once, another sound shatters the night. It takes me a minute to realise what's happening. Everybody looks around, wondering if it's part of the performance.

Mrs Dunstanburgh comes to the front and claps her hands for attention.

'I'm sorry everyone,' she shouts over the din. 'That's the fire alarm. Please proceed outside in an orderly fashion.'

We head outside, sniffing the air for fire.

Clara and the rest of the cast are led out through the side door since the staff are still accountable for them so we stand around near the other parents, while Taylor does her best to look as though she's not with us.

A while later, we are given the all clear and the shepherds stand at the door and usher us in with their crooks.

We return to our seats and wait as the teachers count their charges. There are a few less parents now, I notice. I think some of them nipped to the pub. The performance continues with Clara's solo. She's lost a bit of her bounce as she walks up the steps and reclaims her place at the front. She looks down at us and I give her a big, encouraging smile. She looks out at the audience and begins to sing. She nails it for a second time.

Then the play switches to the stable. Mary yawns widely as she shows off the baby Jesus, then Joseph takes over as she leans back against the hay. The donkey takes centre stage to tell us the play is over and to thank everyone for coming.

Howard and I rise from our seats, clapping enthusiastically. Other parents follow our lead and get to their feet too. Taylor darts a look around to make sure no one's watching. To be fair, there aren't many teenagers here. It's not like anyone's going to spot her. I start to tell her this when I see her staring at the back of the hall.

They fill the back row. All six of them.

And I know immediately what set off the fire alarm. Not what, who.

Howard looks outraged.

'How did they get in?'

I look around. I'm pretty sure they weren't here for the first half. They must have slipped in after the fire alarm. No one was checking the tickets then. Anyone could have come in.

Howard looks uncharacteristically solemn, and I have a horrible feeling he's going to confront them.

'Take a picture,' I tell him instead.

But as soon as he whips out his camera, the girls get to their feet and leave, and by the time we reach the back of the hall, they are out of sight.

'Should we call the police?' Howard says.

'They've gone already,' Taylor says. She looks close to tears.

I want to wrap my arms around her, but I know she'd hate that.

There's a fifteen minute pause while we wait for Clara to get changed. Other parents smile and congratulate us on her performance. I smile back and tell them their children did great too, but those girls have taken the shine out of evening. How dare they show up tonight?

How dare they?

Clara is the last to emerge from the changing rooms, and she is still wearing her star costume.

'What have you been doing?' I ask as I hug her.

'I was helping the others get changed. Then I decided not to change because this is the best costume in the world and I'm going to miss it.'

'Don't you need to give it back?'

'Mrs Dunstanburgh said I could return it after the Christmas holidays.'

'That's very nice of her.'

We step out of the hall and into the cold, dimly lit car park. The six girls are there, perched on the low wall like crows, waiting for us.

My stomach tightens, but I keep my voice steady. 'Take Clara to the car,' I tell Taylor, holding out the keys.

Taylor doesn't move. It's like they've built a force field and she can't step through it.

In the end, Clara reaches for her hand and drags her away.

The girls watch them go, their eyes sharp and unblinking.

I take a breath and walk towards them.

'You've got some nerve showing up here tonight,' I say.

The eldest girl meets my gaze and laughs.

'You've got a nerve,' the girl beside her repeats. Then another joins in. And another. Soon, all six of them are chanting my words back at me like parrots, their voices rising and overlapping, echoing around the car park.

I turn my back on them and walk towards the car.

Howard doesn't follow. 'Leave my family alone,' I hear him say in a firm voice. 'Leave my family alone,' the words echo around the car park.

We get in the car and sit there for a moment, looking at them.

I start the engine and they hop off the wall. They walk into the middle of the lane and spread out, blocking my path.

'Oh, don't tempt me!' I shout.

I glance in the rear-view mirror, then slam the car into reverse. The tires screech as I speed backward, whipping around the corner with a sharp turn. The sudden manoeuvre catches them by surprise, and they all gawp. Without missing a beat, I shift into drive, whiz around them and accelerate away.

'What, never seen someone drive before?' I shout out the window, the triumph bubbling out of me as we leave them behind.

I grip the wheel tighter, the adrenaline coursing through me like fire.

FOURTEEN
JOY

THE HOUSE IS SILENT when I wake up on Saturday. Howard is still fast asleep as I reach for my dressing gown and make my way to the bathroom.

I see they're already out there.

The morning light paints their freckled skin in cold tones, sharpening their hollow-eyed stares.

I dress quickly, pulling on jeans and a jumper. Then I slip out the back door and cross the garden to the house next door. Laszlo isn't a big talker, but he's friendly enough and I've always suspected he'd know what to do in a crisis. I knock briskly, shoving my hands into my pockets to keep them warm.

There's no answer.

I knock again, louder this time, but still, nothing.

'He's gone to visit his parents,' says a voice from the other side of the fence.

I look up to see his neighbour. She has her hair in rollers and she's wearing extra-thick glasses, seventies style.

'Oh. I'll try again later.'

'He'll be a while. They live in Borneo.'

Dammit.

I nod and thank her then slump back to my own house. I head into the kitchen to make coffee. The girls are still there, watching through the window. I pull the blinds.

For goodness sake, I can't hear myself think.

The girls stay out there all day, like a big grey cloud that refuses to drift away, and we're all on edge. Even Clara keeps sneaking peeks out of the window, despite me telling her not to.

I call the police and they send a patrol car round after lunch, but it does no good. The girls scatter as soon as it arrives, only to reappear as soon as it's gone. Howard keeps himself busy fixing a leaky tap, while I do the housework. I am in the middle of hoovering the stairs when Taylor stomps down.

'Right, I've had it!'

I switch off the hoover. 'Are you okay?'

'I'm sick of staying indoors. I'm going to Lucy's.'

'Taylor, wait—'

But she's already slipping into her boots and throwing on her coat.

We watch as she steps out into the street. She doesn't look at the girls. She heads past them, walking so fast she's almost running. The girls all turn and look at her as she passes, like flowers towards the sun.

I hear them all hissing like swans.

'Bitch. Bitch. Bitch....'

Their voices rise and fall in a wave, each one taking up the chant in turn.

I clench my fists, torn between anger and fear. I want to go out there, to shout at them. I want to slap their stupid faces, but I don't. Instead, I reach for my notebook and write it down.

'At least they're not throwing eggs,' Howard says.

'I think they're out of eggs.'

Taylor makes it to the end of the road without incident. Then I spot a police car on the corner. Maybe that's why they let her pass.

Clara dresses her dolls in their swimming costumes and pretends the bathtub is a swimming pool. She puts some tropical music on and sets up a slide. It all looks great fun, I think, peering in at her. I wish I was a doll.

Later, Taylor texts to say Lucy's family is going out for dinner, and she'll be heading home.

'I'll go and meet her at the tube station,' Howards says.

I watch from the kitchen window as he sets off. He's such a kind man, gentle to a fault. The thought of anyone hurling abuse at him makes me feel sick.

I open the window a crack, just enough to hear what's happening but they let him pass without a word.

'Mummy, can I have a biscuit?'

I turn and see Clara.

'Just one. I don't want you to ruin your dinner.'

She goes to the biscuit tin and takes out two. 'I said one!' I remind her.

'I am taking one. The other one is for Emily.'

I look at the doll in her hand and shake my head. 'Emily's already had one.' I tell her.

Clara puts back the second biscuit and hops up onto the counter. The police car has left now. I wait for Taylor and Howard to reappear.

The chanting starts as soon as they come into view:

The youngest starts it, her voice high and mocking, and then it spreads, a creepy wave of sound:

'Daddy's girl. Daddy's girl. Daddy's girl.'

Howard doesn't react. He walks steadily beside Taylor, his shoulders set, head high. By the time they reach the house, the chanting has died down, but the girls remain, watching with unblinking eyes as Taylor and Howard step inside. He locks the door after them and slides the bolt across. Taylor is already ransacking the kitchen. I hear Clara yelp, and the sound of cupboards opening and closing.

'I'd better check on her,' I say, but before I do, Howard pulls me into his arms and holds me for a moment, his heart beats syncing with mine.

'When is all this going to end?' I ask.

He shakes his head. 'They'll get bored of it sooner or later.'

'But what if they don't?'

FIFTEEN
TAYLOR

LUCY'S HOUSE SMELLS LIKE pine needles and cinnamon, with Christmas songs playing in the background. Her mum's gone really overboard with the decorations. Everything shimmers with tinsel or fairy lights. Clara loves it. She probably thinks we're in fairyland.

'Look at all the food,' Lucy says.

The table is practically groaning under the weight of it all: pigs in blankets, sausage rolls, mince pies and bowls of crisps.

'Leave some for the guests,' Lucy's dad says, as if we're even going to make a dent.

'Come on, let's go up to my room,' Lucy says. We each grab a mince pie and head up the stairs.

I sit on Lucy's beanbag and try to pay attention as she tells me about the boy she met at the library.

'He goes to St Gustav's,' she says.

I pull a face. St Gustav's is a lot bigger than our school and has a bit of a reputation. Last year, there was a fight between some of our first years, and some of there's. After that, we were all warned to stay away from them.

'He's nice,' Lucy says, a dreamy look on her face. 'Really funny and clever. He asked if I wanted to go to the cinema with him next week.'

'Cool. What are you going to see?'

'I don't know, whatever's on. Hey, why don't you come too? I could ask him to bring a friend.'

I pull a face. 'Thanks, but I don't want some charity date.'

'It wouldn't be a charity date. You might actually have fun.' She peers at me closely. 'You haven't been much fun lately.'

'Well, thanks a lot!'

'Don't be like that. I'm worried about you.'

'I'm fine, I'm just PMSing.'

I can tell she doesn't believe me, but I don't want to get into it.

'Can we just do something fun?' I ask. 'I thought this was meant to be a party?'

Lucy grins. 'Let's see if we can get something to drink. Mum and Dad bought so much beer and wine I'm sure they wouldn't notice if we borrowed a couple of bottles.'

I smile. 'That's more like it...'

Lucy slides into the kitchen and returns, pockets bulging. We leg it up the stairs, then we discover that the beers need some kind of opener.

'Oh come on!' Lucy says.

We head back downstairs and Lucy is immediately drawn into a boring adult conversation with one of her neighbours. I hear Clara and Bess in the play room. Their voices are low, but there's an intensity that makes me pause. I push the door open a little and peek inside.

Clara and Bess are sitting cross-legged on the carpet. Bess is holding up a spoon and demonstrating something on a large teddy bear.

'You've got to really dig in,' Bess says. She mimes the motion with the spoon. 'Scoop it out like this.' She shows Clara how to dig the bear's eye out with the spoon.

Clara frowns, her brow furrowed in concentration. 'But what if I don't have a spoon?'

'Then you have to use your thumbs,' Bess says. She demonstrates on the bear, digging her thumbs beneath his plastic eye.

Clara tries to copy her but Bess isn't satisfied.

'You're not doing it right.' Bess says. 'It's better with the spoon. Here, I'll show you.'

She leans over Clara, and digs the spoon into the edge of Clara's right eye as if she's attempting to scoop it out.

'Don't!' Clara says, flinching but Bess is holding her down.

'What the hell do you think you're doing?' I growl, stepping into the room.

Clara looks at me with wide-eyed panic but Bess is grinning.

'Just practicing,' she says.

'Practicing what?'

'Self-defence,' Clara says. 'If a man attacks you, you've got to kick him in the balls. And if a woman grabs you, you have to gouge her eyes out.'

My mouth drops open.

Bess holds up her hands, her thumbs poised as if ready to attack Clara's face again.

'Jesus Christ! Bess, put your hands down. Don't practice on Clara.'

Bess lowers her hands, but there's still a devilish glint in her eyes that makes me wonder what she'll do next.

'Where did you even hear about this stuff?' I ask.

'TikTok,' Bess says.

'Right well I don't ever want to see you practicing that on a real person again, do you understand?'

'Whatever,' Bess says.

'I mean it. Or I'll tell your mum.'

Bess actually laughs.

SIXTEEN

JOY

THE AROMA OF MULLED wine drifts through the air as Aimee's husband, Gio stirs the pot in the kitchen. Taylor and Lucy have already headed upstairs when Bess appears to claim Clara. Bess is a year younger than Clara, but already towers over her. She's been a handful since she was a toddler. A menace, to be quite blunt. But she'll grow out of it. At least, that's what I keep telling Aimee, because there's only so much you can do as a parent. They are who they are. I should know - my two are like chalk and cheese.

Gio emerges from the kitchen, handing out the mugs of mulled wine. Howard is driving tonight, so I take one. It has a wedge of orange floating on top.

'Everything looks lovely,' I tell Aimee and I mean it. She's gone to so much trouble. I don't know where she gets the energy. We've only just got our tree up.

I know most of the other guests. There are a few of Aimee's neighbours and several school mums. I watch Clara and Bess out of the corner of my eye. Clara's dolls stay in her bag, I notice. Maybe she's afraid Bess will break them.

'Don't they play nicely together?' Aimee says, tucking her wispy brown hair behind her ear.

I grimace. Aimee is not completely delusional but I think she's just relieved that someone will play with Bess.

I shoot Clara a smile and she returns it to let me know she's coping. She's a good girl, really. I'm not sure I would have tolerated someone like Bess at her age.

Our husbands are deep in conversation. I watch as Gio runs his hand through his thick crop of chestnut curls. He's very talkative, but that suits Howard, who is happy to listen. It's fun to watch as he punctuates his words with a variety of hand gestures. Bess has similar mannerisms and I wonder if he was also a hothead when he was young.

'Can we put on some dance music?' Bess asks.

Aimee hands Bess her phone, and Bess switches on the disco ball, then she and Clara prance about under the lights. Clara looks like she's having fun now, as they raid Bess's dressing-up box and twirl around in long, flowing skirts. Relieved, I turn my attention to Aimee, who is unwrapping the trays for the buffet.

She's put together an impressive spread. There are turkey sandwiches, mini pizzas in the shape of Christmas trees and sugary mince pies. She's even made an American pumpkin pie.

'I got the recipe from a magazine,' she says proudly.

I'm not sure about it but I take a piece, anyway.

'It's very sweet,' I say uncertainly.

'Oh, yes, that's how it's supposed to be,' says Aimee, drowning hers in custard.

The girls get tired of dancing and flop down on the sofa together, both of them dripping with sweat. I watch as they head back into the playroom.

'They'll probably be watching The Little Mermaid,' Aimee says. 'Bess is obsessed.'

I nod, and try to tune out the other school mums. They are all such active parents. Between them, they are petitioning the council for more street lights, carrying out safety patrols of the park and organising litter picks around the school. I feel guilty as I realise I haven't got involved in any of these causes. I've been so consumed with my own life lately, I haven't had much enthusiasm for anything else.

Aimee's neighbours thank her for the party and head home to put their baby to bed, and then the school mums drift away one by one, until it's just our two families left.

Taylor and Lucy clop down the stairs. They have clearly been experimenting with heavy eye make up and have sequins at the corners of their eyes.

'You look like you're going trick or treating,' Gio teases them.

Lucy throws her dad a look, but she doesn't seem to mind. She and Taylor inspect the food table. As Taylor cuts herself a slice of the yule log, there is a tap at the window. I look up, assuming it's one of the school mums back again.

To my horror, the six girls are out there. They line up in height order along the window, peering in.

Taylor drops her paper plate and takes a big step back.

'I don't believe it!'

'Who the hell are they?' asks Aimee.

'Those are the girls who've been stalking us,' I say. 'Hanging around our house and the school.'

'You're joking?' Gio says, straightening from his chair.

'Afraid not. It's been going on for a couple of weeks. We've had to call the police and report them. They must have followed us here.'

Howard's forehead wrinkles. 'How? We came by car.'

'Then they must have a vehicle.'

'Are they old enough to drive?'

'The oldest one might be.'

Aimee looks fascinated. 'And what do they do, exactly?'

'Mostly, they just stand there and chant things. Sometimes they throw eggs. And I think they set off the alarm at the nativity.'

'Well, they better not throw any eggs at my house,' Aimee says. 'I've just washed these windows.'

'So what do we do about them?' Gio asks.

'We'll make a new entry in our log,' Howard says with a sigh.

'I think we can do better than that,' Gio says with a smile.

'What are you going to do?' I ask.

'Just wait there.'

He goes into the mud room and comes back with a large bucket.

'Gio...don't!'

He fills it with water at the sink, then heads for the door. I can barely look.

There's a loud sloshing sound as he pours water all over them. Aimee laughs, but not for long because the girls turn and stare at us again. Even soaked to the skin, they appear calm and collected. I think that's what freaks me out the most.

'Out. Out. Out.' I hear them chant. 'Die. Die. Die.'

When Gio comes back in. There's a swagger to his walk, and a wide grin on his face. He has no idea what he's just unleashed.

The sound of breaking glass shatters the night. Followed by the sharp blare of a car alarm.

'They better not have!' Gio shrieks.

We all race to the door. Gio throws it open and I peer over his shoulder.

Straight away, I see the trail of glass shards, reflecting in the moonlight like shattered diamonds.

My chest tightens, anger and fear twisting into a nauseating knot.

I scan the road but the girls have already fled. Or perhaps they're just hiding in the bushes. It's hard to tell.

'You stay here,' I tell Taylor, as Gio checks his car.

'It's fine,' he says, sounding relieved.

We cross the street to where we parked our car. The windows are gone, every single one. Even the sunroof is cracked and caved in.

We all stand there, staring in stunned silence. My poor car.

Howard pulls out his phone and rings the police.

The police arrive within half an hour, two proper officers this time, not the community support ones from before. Their presence is solid and no-nonsense. They refuse Aimee's offer of a mince pie, and take statements, pens scratching across their notebooks.

'What can you tell us about these girls?'

'I didn't recognise them. Do they go to St Gustav's?' Aimee asks.

I shake my head. 'I wish I knew. They seem to know everything about us. And we know nothing about them.'

Howard squeezes my hand, his grip firm but his face pale.

I tell them again about the CCTV footage at the Riverwood Centre.

The police tell us the same things the other lot did.

'Yeah, we'll look into that. Make sure you keep a log and record everything.'

Like we haven't heard that before.

'What are we supposed to do with this log once it's finished?' Howard asks.

'It's evidence,' the policeman says. 'It will support your case if we manage to apprehend them.'

If.

I don't like the sound of that.

Where is all this going to end?

SEVENTEEN
JOY

'I'll drive you home,' Gio offers, after the police leave.

But he can't. He's been drinking. We look at each other.

'Don't worry, we'll get an Uber,' Howard says.

Clara is weirdly excited about this. She does a little jig to celebrate.

When the Uber arrives, she seems disappointed there are no free drinks or snacks in the back. 'Why is it so small?' she asks loudly.

The Uber driver looks a bit put out. 'This is a seven seater,' he tells her.

'I've seen Ubers on TV and they're very long and stretched,' Clara says.

'No, you're thinking of limos.'

Clara thinks about this for a minute. 'You should drive a limo. They're really cool.'

'Thanks, I'll think about it.'

Taylor stares out the window. I wonder if she's feeling guilty because this all started with her. We arrive back home and I put Clara to bed. She lines her dolls up next to her and I hear her colluding with them as I turn out the light.

'Let's wait till they're all asleep and we'll go down and raid the biscuit tin. We can have a midnight feast.'

I don't worry about it. Clara sleeps like a log. There's no way she's going to be getting up in the middle of the night. Plus, she's scared of werewolves.

I close her curtains and check that there's no one out there. Then I head downstairs and prise the lid off the Christmas sherry. I'll have to buy some more when I do my weekly shop. Aunt Dorothy will be pissed off if there's none left for Christmas.

In the morning, I go online and try to find out more about the girls. We don't have a lot to go on. I try searching the local community boards on Facebook to see if there's been any mention of a gang of girls in our area, but I can't find any references that match our experience.

I can't believe we're the only ones who have been targeted. There must be others out there. Other victims. If only I could find them, they might have some words of advice, or even just help us identify them. That would be a start.

I think for a moment, then I type out a post. I write and delete it a couple of times, feeling unsure of myself.

'If anyone has been affected, I would really appreciate it if you would send me a personal message. You don't have to post publicly.' I type.

But what if the girls themselves see my post? I don't want them to know they've got me so rattled, and I certainly don't want to invite any further repercussions.

Clara peers into our room.

'We've got mice,' she announces.

I sit up straight. 'What do you mean?'

'There was one in the biscuit tin.'

Howard and I look at each other. I put on my slippers and head downstairs, bracing myself for a potential rodent sighting. But what I find is far worse. I spot two of the creatures, scurrying around the kitchen. And they are not the little field mice I'd imagined. They are greyish brown with scaly tails.

'Not mice, rats,' Howard says grimly.

We stare at them in horrified silence. The rats are big, their beady eyes glimmering in the dim light. They are so fast, it's like they work on turbo speed.

'Aw, can we keep them?' Clara asks, from behind us.

'Clara, get back to your room,' I shriek, without taking my eyes off the invaders.

A third one jumps out of the sink and scales down the cupboard door, skidding down towards the floor. It comes barrelling towards us and I scream and jump high in the air. The noise must scare the rat because it charges back the other way and disappears under the fridge.

Taylor comes thundering down the stairs, clutching her cricket bat.

'What's going on?'

Then she sees the rats and screams even louder than I did.

There's no door to our kitchen. You can walk directly from there through to the living room. Which means there's no way to stop them getting out into the rest of the house.

I turn and see Howard leaning against the banisters. He's gone a bit green.

'Let's get out of here,' he says. 'We'll call pest control from the car.'

But of course, our car is still at Aimee's.

'Let's go next door,' I say, looking for my handbag. 'Clara! Get down here!'

Howard is shaking his head. 'No, the old folk will be terrified. And what if the girls are out there?'

I peer outdoors. I can't see any sign of them, but they could still be lurking.

'New plan,' I say. 'Everybody change out of your PJs and we'll go out for breakfast.'

I throw on a jumper and jeans. Then I head downstairs and risk one more look around the kitchen. Immediately, a rat appears from under the fridge and darts under the table. I shudder and take a deep breath before surveying the rest of the room for more signs of infestation. My stomach churns as I spot a few smaller rats chasing each other around the draining board.

I can't wait to get the hell out of here.

Ten minutes later, we head outside. I scan the road, but the girls are nowhere to be seen. We cross the road just as a bus pulls up at the stop. Taylor produces her bus pass while Howard and I search our pockets for change.

'Where to?' the driver asks.

Howard and I look at each other. We hadn't even decided on a destination.

'Balham High Street,' Taylor says.

I nod, 'Yes, High Street please.'

I pay and follow the girls up to the top deck, my eyes sweeping the seats to make sure the gang is not up here because there is no way I'm sitting through a bus journey with them.

I call pest control from the bus. Luckily, our neighbours have our spare key, so I arrange for it to be collected from them, and we head into Balham for breakfast.

'Do you think it could be a coincidence?' Howard asks. 'This sudden rat infestation.'

'No chance,' I snort.

I turn and look out the window. It's a cool crisp morning and we ought to be making the most of our weekend, not fleeing the house in a panic. I think of those creatures scuttling around my clean kitchen and it makes me so angry, I could burst.

How did they even get into our house? I think I already know the answer. There's an old cat flap in the kitchen. I didn't think it was a problem, despite the odd visit from Muppet next door. I didn't think we needed to do anything about it. But it's just the right size for those girls to post things through. Like a family of rats.

In the seat in front of me, Taylor puts on her headphones and stares out the window. There's a futility in her expression, as though she knows there's nothing she can do to stop them. I clench my fists in fury. This vendetta of theirs is getting expensive: busses, Ubers, meals out. Not to mention the glass repairs for our car windows. And now we're going to have to spend the whole day out of the house while the pest control people deal with the rats.

The bus comes to a halt and we all jump off. Taylor points out her favourite diner, and we head towards it. We sit around the table and I try to pretend that we are just out for a family brunch. I paste a smile on my face and Howard does the same. We order lots of food and let the girls order sugary drinks. They deserve a treat, after what we've been through.

'I need the loo,' Clara announces, as we wait for our food to arrive.

'I'll go with her,' Taylor offers.

I shoot her a smile. 'Thanks.'

As soon as they disappear into the ladies, Howard looks at me. 'I'm not going to let those girls ruin our Christmas,' he says.

I lean on my elbows. 'Well, what are we going to do? We can't afford a holiday. We're already overspent, after buying the girls' presents. And there's no way I'm spending Christmas at Dorothy's.'

He looks at me, his expression heavy with defeat. 'The way things are going, we might not have a choice.'

EIGHTEEN
JOY

THE HOUSE GREETS US with a strange, cloying smell as soon as we step inside. It isn't strong, but it's wrong, lingering just enough to make my stomach twist. I stop in the doorway, scanning the dim hallway ahead. The air feels heavy, thick with something I can't quite place.

'I think it's fine,' Howard says behind me, but he hesitates too, his foot hovering over the threshold, and I know he's waiting for me to take the lead.

'Fine?' I glance back at him. 'It stinks.'

Clara, half-asleep on his shoulder, stirs and lifts her head. 'I can't smell anything.'

'That's because you're blocking your nose with Emily's face,' Taylor mutters, brushing past us to head upstairs without so much as a glance. She's been glued to her headphones all day, a protective barrier that's starting to fray my nerves.

I glance after her but decide it's not worth the fight. I need to focus on the rats—or rather, the lack of them. I leave my shoes on as I step inside, unwilling to let my bare feet touch the floor.

The hallway looks the same as it always does: a row of shoes lined up haphazardly against the wall, Clara's star costume hanging off the banister where she left it. But now everything feels different, like I'm walking into someone else's home.

I stand in the kitchen doorway and flick the switch. White light fills the room, turning the counters into cold slabs. The room is silent. Too silent. My ears strain for the tiniest sound—the scratch of claws, the rustle of fur—but there's nothing.

No movement.

No droppings.

No rats.

Still, I can't relax. My eyes flick to the fridge, remembering the way one of them darted under it the last time we were here. My skin prickles at the thought. I edge closer, gripping the counter as I peer down, but the floor beneath is clean.

'Is it safe?' Howard calls from the doorway.

I straighten, turning towards him. 'It looks clean, but I'll need to check properly. The exterminators said the poison would work, but I don't trust it.'

He shifts Clara higher on his shoulder, her little legs dangling as she rides him around the house.

'Giddy up Daddy!'

I move to the windows. The December cold pours in, biting at my skin. I open the back door for good measure, ignoring the shiver that runs through me. Then I spend the next couple of hours deep cleaning the kitchen. I hate the thought that those vermin were in our house, but at least they are gone now, unlike the girls. I finish the cleaning and head into the living room to relax. Howard brings me a cup of tea but as I reach for it, the doorbell chimes, piercing the quiet.

I jump, my heart thudding, and move to the peephole. The sight of the windscreen repair woman is a welcome relief.

'Thanks so much for bringing it over,' I say, pulling the door wider and glancing past her into the street. The shadows feel closer now, heavier. 'I really appreciate it. I know this isn't part of your job.'

She smiles, shrugging. 'Not a problem. It's nice to get out for a bit.'

Her cheerfulness makes me uneasy. She has no idea what she's just walked into.

'Are you alright getting home?' Howard asks, joining me at the door.

'Yeah, my bus is due in a couple of minutes,' she says, pulling out her phone.

'Great. Thanks again,' he replies, giving her a warm nod as she turns to leave.

We stand together, watching as she crosses the street and sits at the bus stop. The orange streetlights spill over her as she scrolls through her phone. For a moment, everything feels normal.

Then the girls appear.

They emerge from the shadows at the end of the road, moving as one. Their voices are low at first, their laughter barely audible. Then one of them nudges the eldest, and lets out a laugh and the sound carries, sharp and mocking.

'Howard.' My voice is tight as I reach for his arm.

We watch as they approach the bus stop, their heads tilting towards each other. The repair woman is oblivious, still scrolling, completely unaware of the predators closing in.

'We need to warn her,' I say, fumbling for my phone. I search for her number but before I can dial, the bus arrives.

The girls pause at the kerb, watching as she boards. They don't follow, and a knot of tension unravels in my chest.

'I'll feel better when she's out of sight,' I say, watching as the bus pulls away.

Howard takes my hand. 'Looks like she's safe. Wish I could say the same for us.'

The youngest girl is holding a stuffed animal by the tail.

It looks like a giant rat.

NINETEEN

JOY

I FINISH MY COFFEE. Howard has just left to drop Taylor at the breakfast club, and Clara is supposed to be getting dressed for school, but instead, I hear her thundering up and down the stairs like a herd of elephants.

As I get up from the table, I notice a message pop up on Facebook. I read with interest.

'You asked about a gang of girls. I think you're talking about the Callaghan family. They used to live in a caravan in somebody's garden on our estate. We thought they were there for a holiday, visiting relatives, but days turned into weeks and it felt like they were never going to leave. There were fights between them and some of the locals. They were a nuisance, playing music late at night, leaving litter, that sort of thing. They were fond of starting bonfires, stinking up the place with their rubbish, but most people didn't dare confront them, and those that did, well let's just say it didn't go well. The police were called out to deal with them a couple of times, but the situation never got any better. Then, just as suddenly as they'd arrived, they moved on. I came home from work one day and they weren't there anymore. I was delighted, but a few months later I saw them again at Riverwood, so clearly they're still around. I wish you luck with them. Those girls will try the patience of a saint.'

I stare at the message. It's comforting to hear that other people have clashed with them, but it doesn't sound like this woman was subjected to anything as bad as what we've had to deal with. For her, the Callaghans were merely a nuisance. For us, it's personal.

I peer outside. There's no sign of them, but that's no comfort. For all I know, they could be hanging around outside Taylor's school. If Howard spots them, he'll call the police. I've told Taylor to tell a teacher if she sees them there again, but she's still being quite coy about it. I think she's embarrassed.

I glance at my watch. 'Clara, you've got ten minutes!' I yell up the stairs, loud enough to compete with the clatter of her toys. Her bedroom door slams. I picture her racing to pull on her school uniform, probably inside out.

Satisfied, I turn back to my phone, scrolling through emails I don't want to deal with and news updates I won't remember later. The morning rush is always the same—stressful and predictable in equal measure.

Once Clara's finally ready, I bundle her into the car with her backpack half-open and her coat flapping behind her like a cape. The school drop-off is mercifully quick today. I give her a kiss on the cheek and get a cheerful, 'Bye, Mum!' before she vanishes into the playground.

As I pull away, my mind shifts to work, mentally running through everything I need to get done. But as I drive back down the high street, I spot three familiar figures walking up the road.

My hands tighten on the wheel. Even from a distance, I recognise them: the tall, wiry one with the dark ponytail leads the way, the two medium-sized ones trail behind.

My heart pounds. They look so ordinary, just teenagers trudging up the road, chatting. But I know better.

They're not harmless.

Not to me.

I study them carefully. There's always been six of them when they've come to taunt us. Strength in numbers and all that. Three on their own are weaker.

More vulnerable.

I'm supposed to take the next left for work, but I keep going, unable to help myself. My hands grip the wheel tighter as I trail them up the high street. It's not hard to keep them in sight with the traffic crawling along.

They reach a precinct of small shops. One of those little clusters with a newsagent, a chippy, and a pet shop. They duck into the newsagent.

I pull into the nearest parking space, heart thumping, and wait. Minutes drag by before they reappear, clutching packets of crisps and steaming hot dogs wrapped in foil. They stand around laughing too loudly, eating, and shoving each other like they own the pavement.

I keep my distance, watching as the eldest, the wiry girl with the high ponytail, suddenly stiffens. Her laughter cuts off mid-sentence, and she starts looking around, sharp and focused.

Her eyes scan the street—left, right, up, and down—like she's trying to sniff out trouble. My stomach flips. I sink lower in my seat, holding my breath, willing myself invisible.

Please don't spot me. Please.

Her gaze lingers on the car park for a fraction too long, and my chest tightens. I fumble for my phone, pretending to scroll, my fingers trembling. She finally looks away and I exhale, still keeping one eye on them as they finish their food and toss the empty packets onto the ground. Finally, they move on again, rounding the corner and heading down a long residential road.

They walk at a snail's pace, chatting and kicking at loose stones on the pavement. It's maddening. I crawl along behind them, knowing how suspicious I must look to anyone who spots me, but I can't lose them.

They pass a football field and walk on in the direction of a large council estate. I think this must be where they are going. I make a decision. I drive past them, and into the estate, where I find somewhere to park.

The estate is quiet. I assume most people are either at work or school. I take a moment to collect myself, glancing around. It's not what I expected. The estate is neat, almost charming, with rows of modern brick houses. There's a small play park in the middle, with swings and a slide. It's surrounded by green spaces. There are benches to sit on and neatly mowed lawns.

I catch myself thinking how nice it all looks. It's not the rundown, grim place I'd imagined. It's the kind of area where kids could play safely and neighbours might actually know each other.

I wouldn't mind living here myself.

But then I remember why I'm here. My focus snaps back to the girls, who are now slowly making their way into the estate, their voices carrying faintly in the distance. I hold my nerve, praying they don't spot me. They walk right past my car, turning into a quiet cul-de-sac with eight houses on each side. They stop at the house at the very end and slip inside without a backward glance.

I take out my phone and note the house number. My hands are shaking. Not with fear, but with satisfaction.

Finally, I'm getting somewhere. I know where they live now. The ball is in my court.

I consider marching up to the door and demanding to speak to their mum. But I stop myself. Not when at least three of them are inside. No, it's better to wait.

The next time they show up at our house, I'll be ready. I'm going to tell their mum exactly what her children have been up to.

TWENTY

TAYLOR

I PUSH THE DOOR open with my shoulder and walk inside. These are the most disgusting loos in the whole school, but I come in here because I like to pee in peace. I head straight for the only usable cubicle and shut the door behind me.

The toilet seat may as well be made of ice, and the loo roll feels like it's made of old crisp packets. But at least there are no Year 10s in here, spraying deodorant and assassinating other girls while they do their make-up.

I flush the chain and walk over to the sink. I turn the tap on, scrubbing my hands quickly under the trickle of water. I look up to check there's nothing weird in my teeth and then I see it:

Bright red letters, smeared across the glass:

'We know it was you.'

My hands freeze under the tap and the water runs down my sleeves.

This wasn't here when I walked in. I would have noticed.

I don't want to look at it, but I can't rip my eyes away. The writing is large and messy. The edges are smudged, bleeding into the glass.

It doesn't say my name.

It doesn't have to.

TWENTY-ONE
TAYLOR

I freak.

The Callaghans are here, in my school.

I grab my bag, sling it over my shoulder, and head out into the corridor. I look left and right. There's a sea of navy blue.

And then I spot her.

The girl stands out, even in uniform. Her jumper clings too tight, and her skirt is too short, the fabric not quite right. She walks down the corridor with a casual air, as if she belongs here, blending into the crowd. But I know better.

My pulse quickens. I think about what to do. I don't think she's seen me yet. I could dart back into the loos, but what if she follows me in there? There would be no way out. Instead, I force my legs to move, slipping into the flow of students heading towards the hall. My breaths are shallow, my skin clammy. The girl turns and looks at me. She smiles like we are old friends.

I spot Lucy just ahead of me, but there's a strict no talking rule in the corridor. Everyone files along in silence. I've got no choice. I turn and knock on the staff room door.

The French teacher comes to the door, eating an apple.

'Yes?'

I cough. 'I... er.' I find myself lost for words. I don't want to tell her. Not if I don't have to. I just want it all to go away.

'I have a sore throat,' I say, feebly.

She looks at me doubtfully. 'Well, you know where the nurse's office is.'

She closes the door again before I can say anything else. The bell rings, and it's time for Spanish. I head straight to the classroom without stopping to fill up my water bottle or check what's on the menu for lunch. For the first time in my life, I'm early.

I keep my eye on the door throughout the lesson. My voice quivers as I practise my Spanish conversation. I'm supposed to be ad-libbing a scene about shopping at a market. Normally, I put a little theatrics into it, but today it's all I can do to summon up the correct sentences.

'It's on the board,' my partner reminds me, when I draw a blank for the second time.

I look at what's written there, but all the words swim together.

'I'm really tired,' I say.

My partner sighs and feeds me the correct response. I repeat it without feeling. Maybe I *should* go to the nurse. I might be able to get out early. I'd feel so much better if I could just get some sleep.

The Callaghan girl is now standing right outside my classroom. I drop my pen on the floor and bend down to retrieve it. I rummage through my bag to make sure I still have the hammer. I stay down there so long, my partner pokes her head down.

'Are you alright?'

'Yeah, I was just...reading graffiti. It's um...in Spanish.'

'Let me have a look.'

Now we're both down here, and it won't be long before the teacher spots us and starts yelling.

I resurface, slowly, cautiously and look over at the doorway.

But she's gone.

TWENTY-TWO
JOY

'STILL FEELING SICK?' I ask, sitting on the edge of the sofa the following morning.

Taylor is curled up under a blanket, pale and subdued.

She shrugs without looking at me.

I touch her forehead. 'You don't feel hot. Are you sure it's not just... everything?'

Her jaw tightens, and she pulls the blanket closer. 'I told you, I'm ill.'

'Alright,' I say softly. 'But you can talk to me, Taylor. You do know that?'

'I really am ill,' she says, turning away.

I sigh and get to my feet. 'Get some rest. I'll be back in a bit.'

I drop Clara off at school, then I drive back, glad it's my day to work from home. As I turn into the street, I see the Callaghans lined up along the bus stop. One of them is eating a flaky sausage roll.

Good.

I pop inside and check on Taylor, who has gone back to sleep. Then I grab my coat and get back in the car, heading straight for the estate.

I park on the road outside their house and walk up the path, practising what I'm going to say. My hand shakes a little as I rap on the door. A dog barks furiously, startling me. I back away as the door creaks open, then smile as a wiry terrier bounds out, yapping at my feet. Such a little dog making all that noise!

'Kingsley!' a voice calls from inside, raspy but commanding. 'Get in here!'

The dog ignores her and goes and sniffs at something in the front garden, while the woman stands there looking dishevelled. I'd guess she's about my age but her greasy hair is grey at the roots and there are dark circles under her eyes. Plus, she's still wearing her dressing gown.

'What do you want?' she says, resting her bulk against the doorframe.

I square my shoulders. 'I need to talk to you about your daughters.'

Her eyes narrow. 'Don't you all?'

I am preparing to launch into my speech when her shoulders droop. 'You might as well come in.'

'Oh – thank you.'

I glance about warily, but there doesn't seem to be anyone else around as I step inside.

'Come on, Kingsley!' she calls, ushering the dog inside.

The hall stinks of stale smoke and the living room is cluttered with dirty plates and empty cans, dog toys scattered across the floor. There is no Christmas tree in this house, no cards or tinsel. Kingsley hops onto an armchair, watching me with bright, curious eyes.

She drops into a chair and immediately lights a cigarette.

I sit opposite, and the dog immediately jumps up onto my lap. I look down at him in surprise. He snuggles up to me like he's known me for ages.

'So what's all this about?' she asks, taking a sip from her mug. I'm pretty sure that's not tea or coffee in there.

'Your daughters have been harassing my family,' I tell her. 'They've vandalised my car and they've been hanging around my house, making threats.'

She exhales a cloud of smoke, shaking her head. 'You think I don't know what they're like?'

I stare at her in wonder. I expected her to deny it, to demand proof. But she doesn't seem the least bit surprised.

Her face softens, and for a moment, she looks almost fragile. She strokes the arm of the sofa, absentmindedly, her fingers trembling. 'They used to be such good girls,' she says quietly.

'What happened?'

She looks at me, her eyes shining with unshed tears. 'Their dad's in prison and their brother died. We've been through hell.' Her voice cracks, and she presses her hand to her mouth.

'That's awful!' I feel tears welling in my own eyes. I don't know what I expected, but it wasn't this.

Tears spill down her cheeks and Kingsley bounds off my lap and onto hers. She strokes him gently and the little dog shifts, licking her hand.

'Rudy, he was the one they listened to. He kept them in line. When he died, they just... stopped caring about anything.'

Her shoulders shake and Kingsley whines softly, nuzzling against her chest.

'I'm so sorry,' I say, my voice low.

She shakes her head, wiping her eyes with the back of her hand.

'Don't be. Sorry doesn't fix anything.' She takes a drag of her cigarette. 'You think I haven't tried? I've begged them, grounded them, everything. But it's like I'm not even here anymore.'

Kingsley barks, as if to protest, and she smiles faintly, scratching behind his ears.

'You're their mum,' I say, desperate to reach her. 'They need you.'

Her laugh is bitter, hollow. 'You think I don't know that? But I'm just...' She trails off, gesturing to herself. 'What am I supposed to do? I've got nothing left.'

I glance up at the picture on the mantelpiece. Seven children, not six. The boy is in the centre. And I can see that he's the focal point, the anchor. The glue that held them together.

She follows my gaze, her fingers still stroking Kingsley's wiry fur. Her voice is low when she speaks, weary but laced with a simmering frustration. 'What would you do?' she asks. 'Some of them are bigger than me, stronger. And none of them listen.'

I hesitate. 'I don't know,' I admit quietly. 'But it's only getting worse.'

She leans back in her chair, her expression hard to read. The little dog shifts on her lap, glancing between us, as if sensing the tension.

'I'm sorry they're causing you grief, but just be thankful you're not in my place.' Her voice is sharp but not unkind.

She looks at me, her eyes tired but searching, as though she's trying to decide if I'm worth her time. She takes another drag of her cigarette and exhales slowly, the smoke curling around her.

I take a deep breath and straighten up. 'Thank you for hearing me out. I hope things get better for you all.'

Her lips twist into a bitter smile. 'And maybe you should consider what your own children have done to provoke my daughters. They don't usually start on someone over nothing.'

I stiffen, but keep my voice calm. 'I don't think that's true. Taylor was just...'

She cuts me off with a sharp look, her tone turning icy. 'Some people think their children's shit doesn't stink.'

The comment stings, but I nod. 'I hear what you're saying.'

She stubs out her cigarette with unnecessary force, then reaches for a mug on the side table. I notice the tremble in her hand as she takes a long sip. Her eyes never leave mine.

When she sets the mug down, her expression darkens, and her voice drops to a warning tone. 'You should leave now. You don't want to make things worse for yourself.'

Kingsley lets out a soft growl, echoing her words.

I nod, my heart racing as I step back toward the door. 'Alright. Thank you for your time.'

I feel her eyes on me as I turn to leave. Hers and the dog's. Solemn and unblinking, just like her daughters.

TWENTY-THREE
TAYLOR

THE HOUSE IS STILL. No TV blaring, no radio talking to itself. No Clara charging about.

I glance at the clock. Clara must be at school. Dad will be at work. And Mum?

I push myself up from the sofa and wonder into Mum's office. The door is open, the desk is clean and uncluttered, her laptop closed, papers stacked in a neat pile. Everything looks exactly as it should. Except she's not here.

I turn back towards the living room, trying to shake the unease. I've been home alone lots of times. Mum and Dad know I'm mature enough to take care of myself for a few hours. Normally, I love alone time. I raid the cupboards and watch what I want on TV. Or else I put my music on full volume and dance around the living room.

It's never been a big deal, up until now.

Then I hear it.

A creak, like a floorboard shifting under weight.

I freeze. My heart skips a beat. It's soft, subtle, but unmistakable.

I tell myself it's nothing—the house settling, maybe. But the silence that follows feels heavy, pressing, as if the walls themselves are holding their breath.

My body tenses and I hiccup.

Another creak. Closer this time.

I take a step back, my pulse hammering in my ears. Someone is here.

I hear a thud as something heavy hits the floor.

I run to the door, my pulse pounding so loudly it drowns out the next sound. I back toward the stairs, my eyes darting to the hallway.

I need my phone.

I bolt up the stairs two at a time, shutting my bedroom door behind me. My hands tremble as I shove my bed against it. I grab my phone from the charger. My breath comes in shallow gasps as I unlock it. My fingers shake so badly it takes two tries to punch in the numbers: 9-9-

'Taylor!'

Mum's voice cuts through the house.

I pause, the phone slipping from my hand.

'Mum! They're in the...'

I stop, pressing my ear to the door. The house is silent again.

No footsteps.

No voices.

Were they scared off by Mum's arrival? That doesn't seem likely. The Callaghans don't scare that easy.

I inch the bed back and crack the door open, peering out into the hallway.

Nothing.

I step out cautiously, my heart hammering in my chest as I creep down the stairs.

Mum is standing at the foot of the stairs.

'Did you break a plate?' she asks.

'What?'

She nods at the kitchen.

'I think it was them,' I say.

A look flashes across her face.

'They're all at the bus stop. I just passed them.'

'But they were here. I'm sure of it.'

She frowns but doesn't dismiss me entirely. Together, we check the house. Every room, every window, every door. Nothing else is out of place. Just that one plate, lying in smithereens on the kitchen floor. Mum sweeps it up and puts the kettle on. We sit at the table, sipping tea together like old ladies.

My hands shake as I hold my cup. They were here. I know they were but how did they get in? And come to that, how did they get out? Without Mum seeing?

I slide to my feet and check the window. Mum's right, they're all standing at the bus stop. I count, just to make sure. One, two, three, four, five, six.

Yup. All accounted for.

I breathe a shaky sigh of relief, but it doesn't last.

They were here. I know they were.

How did they get in? And how did they leave without a sound?

The thought chills me to the bone.

And worse still, what if they come back?

Mum sits me down again, her hands resting lightly on my shoulders. She leans in, peering into my eyes, her gaze unnervingly intense, like she's trying to see straight into my soul.

'You know you can tell me anything?' she says, her voice soft but insistent.

I nod, not trusting myself to speak. I don't want her to say it again. I don't want her to *look* at me like that, like she can fix me if she just tries hard enough.

'I mean it, Taylor.' Her eyes search mine.

I look away, my jaw tightening.

I wish she'd stop saying that. I wish she'd stop looking at me like she *knows*.

I wish they'd all leave me the hell alone.

TWENTY-FOUR

JOY

A STRANGE PONG WAFTS through the air as I head downstairs Thursday morning. It prickles at the back of my throat, the kind of smell that makes you feel a bit sick.

When I head into the kitchen, I see that the freezer door is wide open. A sticky puddle spreads across the floor, streaked with melted ice-cream and flecks of something unidentifiable. Bags of vegetables have split, their contents turning to mush. My carefully stacked containers of lasagne and stew drip onto the shelf below. Ice crystals cling to the edges of the drawers, slowly dissolving into sticky streaks. The unmistakable smell of spoiled dairy and defrosted meat hangs in the air.

I grab a towel and crouch down, wrinkling my nose as the fabric soaks up the mess. It's futile—there's too much water, too much slime. I sling the ruined food in the bin, salvaging what I can for tonight's dinner. The ice cream tub buckles as I lift it, spilling a pale, sugary sludge onto my hand. I swear under my breath and rinse my hands under the tap.

'What are you doing?'

I glance up to see Taylor in the doorway, her eyes flicking between me and the mess.

I straighten up. 'Did you leave the freezer door open?'

Her expression shifts from confused to angry. 'It wasn't me!'

'Well, it didn't open itself,' I say, my patience fraying.

She crosses her arms, her voice rising. 'I bet it was those girls!'

I blink at her, caught off guard. 'Don't be ridiculous.'

'I'm not! I told you—they've been in the house!'

Howard's voice drifts in from the hall. 'What's all the shouting about?'

He appears in the doorway, rubbing his eyes. His gaze sweeps over the puddle and the open freezer.

Taylor appeals to him. 'It was those girls.'

He frowns. 'We can't blame everything on the Callaghans,' he says, his tone maddeningly calm. 'These things happen. Maybe the door didn't shut properly.'

'It wasn't the door!' Taylor shouts, her face flushing. 'I told you they can get in!'

I throw the towel into the sink, my temper flaring. 'Taylor, that's just not possible. The doors were locked, and all the windows were shut.'

'Okay, don't believe me!' She spins on her heel and storms out of the room.

I exhale slowly, the stench invading my nostrils.

Howard steps over the puddle.

'She's scared,' he says quietly.

'She's being ridiculous.'

He doesn't argue, just bends down, scooping up mushy peas with his hands and dumping them into the bin.

'How are you feeling?' Howard asks Taylor as we sit down to breakfast a little later. Taylor reaches for a slice of stollen cake.

Aunt Dorothy would have a fit if she knew we were letting the girls eat cake for breakfast, but I don't care. It's quick and easy, and after the morning we've had so far, it's what we need.

'No better,' Taylor says, barely lifting her head.

I glance at Howard, sharing a quiet look. Taylor's been off school for two days already, and today's the last day of term.

Clara, on the other hand, is practically buzzing, her plate already half-empty. 'We're doing Secret Santa today!' she squeals. 'And the Christmas quiz. Miss Mott said there's going to be prizes. I hope I get one. I hope it's a pop-it. Or a water pistol.'

'That sounds fun,' I say, smiling at her enthusiasm before turning back to Taylor. 'You should go in, Taylor. They'll be doing fun stuff at your school too and you've got the Christmas dinner today.'

Taylor doesn't answer right away. She shakes her head, her mouth set in a stubborn line.

'Come on,' I try again, keeping my tone light. 'It's the last day.'

She looks up, her expression miserable. 'I can't. I don't feel well.'

Howard takes a sip of his coffee. We share a look. We could force her, but what's the point?

'Fine, you can stay off. But you have to tidy your bedroom.'

Taylor doesn't respond, just slumps further into her chair like this is a massive imposition.

She spends the day in front of the TV, flicking between Christmas films. The heartwarming stories don't seem to touch her. She stares blankly at the screen, her chin propped on her hand, her expression as flat as the grey sky outside.

I sit with her for a while, hoping my presence might help, but she doesn't say much. I spread out the wrapping paper and set to work on the last of the presents, the scissors slicing through paper, tape snapping into place. I write out the last of my Christmas cards, my handwriting a little shaky from the tension in my shoulders.

Every so often, I glance at Taylor. Her eyes are glazed, her shoulders hunched. She looks as miserable as a donkey trudging through snow. My chest tightens. I don't know how to reach her. Taylor loves Christmas as much as Clara does. She nagged us to put up the Christmas tree the second Halloween ended, pleading until Howard gave in and hauled the decorations down from the attic. I loved watching her arrange the baubles. Taylor decorated the top of the tree, then crouched down to oversee Clara as she arranged the lower branches. She always loved putting the star on top, but as she's got older, she's handed that honour down to her little sister, lifting her up so she can reach. It always fills my heart with so much joy. I can't bear to think that magic is fading. Now, she just sits there, her face pale in the glow of the TV, and I don't know how to bring her back.

I have a hard time falling asleep that night. My thoughts spiral, circling endlessly around the Callaghans and the chaos they've brought into our lives. I picture their mother, and her hollow eyes. What would I do in her place? Would I fight for my family, or would I too let go of the wheel?

Then I think of the girls themselves, standing across the street, day after day, taking out their misery on us. I wonder what they're thinking, what they're planning. It feels like there is no end in sight.

Sleep finally claims me, dragging me down into its depths like a sinking ship. But it's not restful. My dreams are fragmented, vivid, and disturbing. I see the Callaghans everywhere—in the windows, behind the door, at the foot of my bed. Their laughter echoes in my ears, and I wake, gasping for breath, only to realise I never stopped dreaming.

When I finally slip into a deeper sleep, it feels like only moments before I'm jolted awake. A blast of music shatters the quiet, crashing through the house like a wave.

I freeze. A combination of fear and exhaustion pins me to the mattress. My heart pounds as I try to make sense of it. The noise burrows into my brain.

I recognise the words:

'Three blind mice, three blind mice,
See how they run, see how they run!
They all ran after the farmer's wife,
Who cut off their tails with a carving knife,
Did you ever see such a thing in your life?
As three blind mice.'

My stomach clenches as the words echo in my mind:
For a moment, I can't move. They're not outside anymore.
They're in the house.
'Howard!'
The lyrics repeat, the words cutting through the air: '

'See how they run! See how they run!'

Howard jerks awake beside me, eyes wide and unfocused.

'What the hell is that?' he says, throwing back the duvet.

I hear the soft creak of footsteps outside the door.

We both freeze. I flick on the light, my eyes scanning the room. I grab a slipper from the floor and clutch it tight.

The door handle turns, and the door inches open. The slipper trembles in my hand.

Then Clara appears, her hair messy, Emily dangling from one hand.

'What's happening?' she asks, her voice thick with sleep.

I exhale, dropping the slipper. 'It's okay,' I whisper.

Howard moves closer, his voice firm but calm. 'It's nothing, Clara. Go back to sleep.'

She doesn't move, her wide eyes flick between us as the song continues to play. I reach for her. 'It's fine. Just some music.'

Clara nods, her lip quivering. I guide her back to her room and tuck her in, forcing a smile.

'Stay here, okay? Don't come out, no matter what. Daddy and I are just checking something.'

She nods again, but the look in her eyes guts me. She doesn't believe me, and I don't blame her.

I look in on Taylor. She's still fast asleep.

I find Howard at the top of the stairs, his face set in a grim mask. He doesn't say a word, just grips the banister and starts down into the darkness. The faint glow from the hall light barely reaches the staircase, leaving the shadows thick and impenetrable.

'Careful!' I whisper, my voice tight with fear.

He nods but doesn't pause, his movements slow and deliberate. He's barely taken two steps when his foot slips. For a heart-stopping moment, his arms flail wildly, grasping at the banister but finding nothing to hold on to.

'Howard!' I gasp, my voice louder now, panic surging through me.

He pitches forward, his body twisting as he loses his balance. The dull thud of his back hitting the steps reverberates up the stairwell, followed by the sickening sound of him crashing to the bottom.

.

TWENTY-FIVE
JOY

I FLY DOWN THE stairs after him, realising too late that the steps are wet. I skid, but catch myself and finish the journey on my behind.

Howard groans softly, one hand clutching his side. I drop to my knees, my hands trembling as I reach for him.

'Are you okay? What hurts?'

'I'm fine,' he grinds out through clenched teeth, his voice strained. He starts to push himself up, wincing with the effort.

'Don't move!'

'I'm fine,' he repeats, though the tightness in his voice betrays him. His hand skims over one of the steps as he steadies himself, and I notice the faint sheen on his fingers. It glistens in the dim light.

'What is that?' I ask, leaning closer.

Howard holds up his hand, staring at the slick substance coating his fingertips.

'It that... oil?' His eyes meet mine, and the realisation dawns: Someone did this.

The music stops abruptly, cutting off mid-verse. The silence that follows is worse. Howard clambers to his feet with my help, wincing but brushing me off when I fuss over him. Together, we check the downstairs rooms, both of us on edge. We look in every conceivable place, even the small utility cupboard.

Nothing.

No broken windows. No forced entry. But the freezer door is open again, its frosty interior spilling cold air into the room. I slam it shut, the sharp puff of icy air brushing my face.

I find Howard in the living room, standing over the ancient stereo system his father gave us as a wedding present. He ejects a tape from the deck. The faint mechanical click echoes in the quiet room. He holds it up for my inspection.

I stare at the tape, my stomach sinking. We haven't used that stereo in years, not since streaming took over. I didn't even know it still worked.

'Where did it come from?' I ask, stepping closer.

Howard shakes his head, his jaw clenched. 'I don't know. But they had to have been here. Someone had to put it in.'

Ever so carefully, he sets the tape down on the coffee table as if it might explode.

I hate the thought of those girls sneaking into our house, touching our things, invading our privacy.

'We need to call the police,' I say, my voice firmer now.

Howard looks at me, his lips pressed into a thin line. 'And tell them what? That a group of kids broke in to play a nursery rhyme? You know what they'll say.'

I don't respond. He's right. The police already think we're overreacting, that it's just kids being kids. But this isn't normal. This isn't a prank.

I glance at the tape again.

'They're getting bolder,' I say. 'We have to do something.'

The curtains stir faintly, shifting just enough to catch my eye. My heart skips a beat, but when I move closer, I see the windows are all shut tight. The locks still in place. The cold glass reflects my worried face back at me.

We sink down on the sofa. The Christmas decorations look out of place, their cheerfulness a stark contrast to the feeling in this house.

'They're trying to scare us,' he says, his voice low but steady.

'It's working,' I say through my hands. 'I can't do this. I can't let them ruin Christmas.'

He shakes his head. 'We won't let them.'

'But what's to stop them?'

'We'll go somewhere. Aunt Dorothy's...'

'They'll just follow us there. And I'm not making Dorothy a target. Her heart won't take it.'

'Somewhere else, then. Further away. Where they won't find us.'

'Where then? It's not like we can afford a last-minute getaway. We've already had to fork out for the car repairs.'

I take his arm, steering him gently. 'Come on. Let's get back to bed.'

But I know I won't sleep tonight. Not with them out there, plotting their next move.

Upstairs, I check on Clara. She's curled up in her blankets, her eyes squeezed shut. I kiss her forehead and linger by the door, listening for any sound that doesn't belong. The house is quiet again, but it's not the comforting quiet it used to be.

Howard and I lie awake for ages. Every creak of the house sounds like an earthquake. The air is thick with the expectation of something worse.

'How did they get in?' I ask. 'We have the only keys. Us and...'

We stare at each other, the same thought flickering between us. Margaret next door is the only one with a spare key. She's sweet but dithery. It wouldn't take much to con her. Maybe they've stolen it from her. Or worse, borrowed it and made a copy without her even realising.

Howard shifts, propping himself up on one elbow. 'We'll get the locks changed first thing,' he promises.

I nod, but it doesn't ease the knot in my chest. 'I can't sleep. I'm just lying here waiting for the next thing to happen.'

'I know what you mean.'

The room falls silent. Nothing but the sound of his breathing and mine. It's comforting, in a way, the fact that we are in this together.

The door creaks open. I sit up instinctively, my heart racing, but it's only Clara. She's standing in the doorway, Emily dangles from one hand.

'I can't sleep,' she says, her voice small.

She's too old for this—too old to crawl into our bed—but neither of us says no. Not tonight. I pull back the covers, and she climbs in between us, curling against my side. Howard reaches out, resting a hand lightly on her shoulder.

The three of us lie there, staring at the ceiling, listening to the quiet. Then, one by one, we drift off into uneasy sleep.

TWENTY-SIX
TAYLOR

I HEAR THE MUSIC echoing through the house, but I don't dare get out of bed. I'm too chicken. I lie there, frozen, hiding under my duvet like I did when I was a little kid.

When my door creaks open, I squeeze my eyes shut and play dead. I don't know if it's the Callaghans, or my parents checking in on me. My breath comes in shallow bursts, my chest tight with fear. If it's the Callaghans, I hope they'll make it quick.

I hear a yelp of pain.

'Dad?'

My eyes fly open, and before I can stop myself, I'm out of bed, my bare feet hitting the cold floor as I run to the door. Mum's already there, rushing down the stairs to help him.

I stop in the doorway, my hand clutching the frame, and watch them in horror. Dad is lying at the bottom of the stairs, groaning, and Mum is kneeling beside him, helping him.

The Callaghans did this. I know they did.

I should help them. I should run down there, do something, anything, to make it better. But my legs won't move. My hands tremble, and my throat feels tight, like I can't get enough air. I slip back into my room and close the door behind me as quietly as I can. My heart is racing, and I hate myself for it, but I open the wardrobe and climb in. I curl up at the bottom and stay there.

I'm not a person.

I'm a coward.

I don't come out until everything goes quiet again. Their voices drift up the stairs, soft and hushed, as they try to decide what to do. I want to tell them. I want to scream it at the top of my lungs.

They don't want you. It's me they want. Just hand me over, and all this will go away.

But I can't say it, because then they will hate me.

As much as I hate myself.

I stay in my room for much of the next day. Clara is in and out, bouncing around because it's the Christmas holidays and she's really, really excited.

She wants me to play with her. Dolls, cards. Anything.

I just can't.

My world has turned slushy and grey.

'Can you keep an eye on Clara while I pop out?' Mum asks later that afternoon.

I nod and crawl back into bed.

Clara skips into my room. I open one eye and see a bunch of her dolls sitting in a circle in front of me, reading my books. I can't even crack a smile. I turnover and face the wall. I really am tired. I feel like I'm becoming some kind of nocturnal animal. Awake all night and asleep all day.

I come downstairs much later to find Mum taking the stockings down from the mantelpiece. Dad is pulling the decorations off the tree.

'What the...'

They both turn and look at me. 'Shh! Don't wake Clara.'

My eyes narrow. 'Why are you taking everything down?'

'We're leaving,' Mum says.

'Leaving?'

Mum looks all around, as if she expects to be overheard.

'Our boss has a cabin up in Scotland. It's empty this Christmas, and he's letting us use it. We leave at two in the morning.'

My mouth drops open. 'We're doing a midnight flit?'

Dad's face breaks into a grin. 'I'd rather think of it as a holiday.'

TWENTY-SEVEN
JOY

CLARA'S SINGING FADES AS we push further and further north. Taylor is quiet, staring at her phone. I've warned her to stay off social media. To turn off her snapchat, and check her phone for tracking apps, and yet I'm staring out at the shadowy shapes of hills and trees, unable to shake the feeling we're being followed. It's not logical. We left before dawn, switching routes more than once. And still the unease lingers, pricking at me like the sharp point of a needle.

When we reach the service station outside Birmingham, Howard pulls in without a word. We get out stiffly, stretching legs that feel more like lead than limbs. It's cold. Colder than I expected. Frost clings to the edges of the pavement, and our breath hangs in the air as we shuffle inside.

'Mum, look!' Clara presses her nose against the shop window, pointing at a display of Bliss dolls. One with purple hair stands front and centre, its box pristine and sparkly.

'I see it, darling, but the shop's closed,' I say, tugging her back gently.

'That's the one I want,' she says, her finger smudging the glass.

I rack my brain. Is that the one I bought her? Or did I choose the one with silver hair? I remember standing in the shop with Howard, the two of us debating it while the sales assistant chewed his gum. Clara hadn't mentioned a colour in her letter to Santa so it had been left to us to guess.

When we return to the car, I take the wheel, and Howard slumps into the passenger seat, snoring softly within minutes. The girls fall quiet again as the scenery changes, hills rising like giants in the distance. By the time we reach Northumberland, the clouds hang low and heavy, turning the landscape into a brooding painting.

'Is this Scotland?' Clara asks.

'Not yet,' I say, smiling despite myself.

When we cross the border, everybody cheers. Even Taylor, who has barely spoken since we left, cracks a grin as Howard pulls over near the *Welcome to Scotland* sign. The kids scramble out of the car. The wind is sharp and bracing, but for a moment, I don't care. For a moment, I forget why we're here and let myself enjoy the novelty of an unexpected holiday.

Howard snaps photos as Clara dances around the sign, pulling funny faces. Even Taylor poses reluctantly, her grin more genuine than I've seen in weeks. It feels as though some of the tension has lifted, at least for now.

We stop in a small village to find a pub. A small, local one with a roaring fire and mismatched tables and chairs that seem to have been collected over decades. I'm not sure if this is a late lunch or an early dinner, but nobody minds. Feeling adventurous, we order off the specials board. Taylor eyes the haggis suspiciously, her fork hovering over the plate.

'What even is this?' she asks, wrinkling her nose.

'You don't want to know,' Howard says with a grin.

'More for me!' Clara says, stabbing a chunk with her fork.

Taylor rolls her eyes but doesn't argue. Everyone agrees the chips are good, golden and crispy, and the deep-fried Mars bars are a huge hit.

On the way back to the car, Taylor stops in front of a bright orange VW van parked on the kerb and holds up her phone.

'This is so cool,' she says, angling herself for a selfie.

'Don't post this online.' My voice is sharper than I intended.

She rolls her eyes. 'I'm just sending it to Lucy, if that's okay with you?'

I glance at Howard. 'I suppose there's no harm.'

I pull Clara closer, her small hand slipping into mine as we make our way back to the car.

The holiday-like atmosphere grows as we reach the Highlands. The roads grow narrower, winding through darkening hills and it feels a world away from the congested streets of London.

But this isn't a holiday. Not really. Beautiful as all this is, we shouldn't have had to run away. We should be spending Christmas in our own home. With Aunt Dorothy.

I doze off, despite all Clara's chatter, and when I open my eyes again, we are in Inverness.

'Look out for Nessie!' says Howard.

Clara presses her face against the window, as if expecting the Loch Ness Monster to pop up at any minute.

'Are we nearly there yet?' Taylor wants to know.

'Just a bit further,' Howard says.

As we get closer, I wish I was the one driving. It's both beautiful and treacherous, navigating the narrow roads up into the mountains.

'Are we in the Alps?' Clara asks, as we pass whispering willows dusted with snow.

I burst out laughing. 'It feels a bit like it, doesn't it?'

I've never seen anything so beautiful. The sun is setting, and the colours erupt across snow-peaked mountains. At the end of the road, is a path, and at the end of the path, down a very narrow road, is a wrought-iron gate. There is no name on it. No number. No indication of where we are.

'How do we know if this is the right place?' I ask.

'We don't,' Howard says.

He jumps out and opens the gate, then walks up the drive to ring the bell. No one answers. He locates the key under a large stone griffin and opens the door, waving at us triumphantly.

As we step out of the car, I hear the sound of babbling water from a nearby stream. I breathe in the refreshing scent of the pine trees and I'm instantly transported back to childhood Christmases in Snowdonia. My brother and I were mad about the snow. It always started with a single snowball to the head and escalated to a all out war. We'd build our own snow forts and co-op other children to join our teams. I never seemed to feel the cold back then.

I turn to look at the cottage that will be our home for the next couple of weeks. Whispering Willows is an old style stone building that blends with the natural beauty of the landscape. Clara immediately dives into the woodshed, mistaking it for a playhouse. Howard picks her up and bundles her over his shoulder then carries her inside.

The inside is cosy but cold. Fluffy throws are draped over the backs of the sofas, and the walls are decorated with pictures of woolly Highland cows, their shaggy faces peering out of the frames.

'Look at the fireplace!' Taylor says, her face lighting up as she looks at the massive stone hearth.

It's good to see her smile.

'We'll get that going in a minute.' Howard says.

We explore the cottage. Clara bags the room at the front and positions her dolls on the windowsill so they can see out.

'Right,' says Howard. 'Who wants to help get the firewood?'

'Me!' Clara says, jumping up and down.

I leave them to it, while Taylor and I make up the beds. There is a room for each of them, which I'm really pleased about because often when we go on holiday they have to share, and they end up fighting within five minutes.

'It was good of you to let Clara choose the front room,' I say to Taylor.

She smirks. 'Not really. My room has a mini bar.'

I almost drop the pillow I'm fluffing. 'You'd better be joking.'

She tilts her head and gives me a cheeky smile.

Once the beds are made up, we head downstairs and I get a better look at the kitchen. The cupboards are stocked with tins, pasta and long-life milk, and there is a freezer which contains and entire turkey, Yorkshire puddings, vegetables and roast potatoes. Everything we'll need for tomorrow.

I make hot chocolate for Clara, and tea for the rest of us and we settle in quite nicely, even though Taylor is shocked to find the TV only has five channels. Howard puts up our tree and Taylor and Clara decorate while I hang the stockings over the fireplace.

Outside, the darkness is drawing in, but unlike back home, there are no streetlights to dull the night. The only light comes from the stars, scattered like sequins across the inky expanse. Above the white-capped mountain, the constellations seem sharper, brighter, as though the crisp air has scrubbed them clean. Orion's Belt gleams confidently in its neat line, and the Plough stretches across the heavens, a celestial signpost in the vastness of the sky.

I step outside, wrapping my arms around myself against the chill. I draw in a deep lungful of mountain air and feel my body unwind. Standing here beneath this endless sprawl of stars, I am struck by how small I am—how small we all are—compared to the vastness of the universe.

For a moment, the weight of everything lifts, replaced by the knowledge that, in the grand scheme of things, our troubles are fleeting, and insignificant. The stars twinkle above as though they've been watching for millennia, steady and unchanging, and a fragile tranquillity washes over me, soothing the raw edges of my fear.

When both the girls are in bed, I fill the stockings and arrange the larger presents around the base of the tree. The cottage is quiet except for the crackle of the fire. Outside, the wind howls, sending bursts of snow against the windows.

Howard sits across from me, his elbows on his knees, staring into his hands. There's a deep crease between his brows, the same one he gets when he's solving a problem at the office.

Finally, he exhales and looks up. 'We can't keep this up forever,' he says, his voice low.

I shift in my chair, wrapping my hands around the warm mug in my lap. 'What do you mean?'

'This,' he says, gesturing vaguely around the room. 'Running. Hiding.'

'This was your idea,' I say, confused.

He sighs. 'This is just a temporary reprieve. They're still going to be there when we get back.'

'I know.'

'So I've been thinking. We could sell the house. Start afresh somewhere else. Somewhere they can't find us.'

I tighten my grip on the mug. 'Where?'

'I don't know,' he admits, leaning back in his chair. 'Yorkshire, maybe. It's far enough from London, but close enough we could commute if we needed to.'

I let out a short laugh, but there's no humour in it. 'It's a hell of a commute, Howard. And what about the girls? You want to uproot their whole lives, change their schools, just to run away?'

'To protect them,' he corrects, his eyes meeting mine.

'You really think moving away is the answer?'

'Well, what else can we do? What happens when we go home, Joy? You've seen the way things have been going. The Callaghans are evil. They just don't care. And we've no way of knowing what they're going to do next. If they can't get into our house, they might burn it down or something. Lord knows where all this is going to end.'

His words hit their mark, and I feel my resolve falter.

'I'm trying to protect our family,' he says, softer this time. 'What do you want me to do? Fight them? Take them to court? You know that's not an option.'

'And running is?' I demand, standing up. The mug trembles in my hands, but I don't set it down. I need the warmth, and it's something to hold on to. 'Packing up our lives and starting over because we're too scared to stand our ground?'

His voice cracks, frustration spilling out. 'If that's what it takes to keep us safe, then yes!'

I stare at him, the firelight flickering between us.

He runs a hand through his hair, slumping back into the chair. 'I'm trying to find a way forward,' he says quietly. 'For all of us.'

TWENTY-EIGHT
JOY

I TURN TOWARDS THE window, staring at the snow-covered trees outside. The wind shakes the branches, scattering clumps of white to the ground.

Howard's words swirl in my head, mixing with my own thoughts, my own doubts.

He's right about one thing, we can't stay in this limbo forever. But selling the house? Leaving everything behind? It feels like admitting defeat.

Like letting the Callaghans win.

I think of our daughters.

Those girls have put them through so much already, especially Taylor. How can I ask them to start over somewhere new, to leave behind the life they know because we can't protect them?

'I hate this,' I say, my voice trembling with the effort of holding back tears. 'I hate that they're pushing us out. I hate that we even have to consider it.'

'I know,' Howard says, his voice soft. 'But what's the alternative?'

I turn and look at him, at his good, kind face, and feel a surge of resentment so sharp it stings. I hate myself for it, for wishing, just for a moment, that he were a different kind of man—an alpha male, strong and forceful. The kind no one would dare mess with.

But if he were that man, he wouldn't be my Howard. He wouldn't be the man I fell in love with, the man who balances me when I feel off kilter. I take a shaky breath, my gut twisting inside me.

'We don't have to decide anything tonight,' he says at last. 'Let's go to bed. Lord knows we need some rest.'

I nod, but the knot in my chest doesn't loosen as we head up the stairs and slip into the unfamiliar bed.

The next thing I know, Clara is peering in at us.

'Mum? Dad? It's Christmas!'

I open my eyes, and for a moment, I don't remember where I am. Then I look out the window and see the mountains. It has snowed more overnight. Everything is a brilliant, gleaming white. I reach out and touch the frosty windowsill, marvelling at just how much snow has accumulated. Icicles hang down from the branches of the nearest tree and a thick blanket of snow covers everything in sight. It's like a fantastical winter wonderland. I can barely even make out the car.

'Can you see any hoofprints?' Clara asks.

'What?'

'Well, they must have landed up on the roof.'

I arrange my face into a serious expression.

'There's so much snow, any prints will be completely covered.'

Howard shifts and groans beside me, his arm dangling down to the floor. Clara stands over to him and shakes him gently.

'Wake up, Daddy! It's Christmas!'

A groggy looking Taylor appears in the doorway.

'Well?' she says. 'Are we doing Christmas or what?'

Downstairs, Howard gets the fire going and I take down the stockings and hand them round. We sit round in a circle to open our presents. Howard pulls a pair of socks from his stocking and then an orange. 'Lucky me', he says, looking delighted.

I'm not quite as good at feigning excitement as I open my new hairdryer. Taylor smirks.

'Oh my god, I got a Bliss doll!' Clara shrieks before she's even unwrapped hers. She knows by the feel of the box. She tears into it, and she's right. It's the one with the purple hair. I heave a sigh of relief as she hugs it tight.

'This is the one I wanted! Look, Mummy! I can't believe it. I must have been a really good girl!'

Howard darts a look at me. 'I thought we got her the silver one?' he whispers.

Did we? My thoughts churn, the memory slipping just out of reach. I glance at the doll in Clara's hands—purple hair, sparkly box.

We must have got it right.

'Let's see,' Taylor says. 'Wow, that is a really cool doll, Clara. What are you going to call it?'

'She's not an "it"; she's a "she",' Clara says, 'and I'm going to call her Star.

Taylor doesn't look impressed by the name. Probably, Clara has no idea Star and Taylor are no longer friends. Or perhaps she knows very well and is teasing her sister. It can be hard to tell when she always looks so sweet and innocent, but Clara has her naughty side too.

Taylor scowls, but Clara just hugs the doll tighter. Her grin is in equal parts bright and mischievous.

Taylor turns to her own stocking and starts pulling out something heavy, I try to remember what I put in there. A silver necklace and a set of miniature perfumes. Howard always sneaks extra treats into the girls' stockings, like candy canes, and bags of chocolate sprouts. I really wish he wouldn't. Last year, Clara ate so much chocolate she didn't have room for her Christmas dinner.

I glance at Taylor's hands, trying to figure out what Howard might have snuck in this time. But the longer I look, the less sense it makes. Taylor's expression shifts from curiosity to confusion. She gasps and withdraws her hand, holding it up to the light. Streaks of what looks like red paint run down her fingers. It's everywhere, on her palm, her wrist, even pooling on the rug beneath her.

My stomach drops. 'Taylor, what...?'

But before I can finish, she puts her hand back in and pulls the object carefully from the stocking. It's only then I see the jagged edge, and the cruelly pointed tip. The blade glints as blood runs down its length, dripping onto her lap.

'Oh my God!' she cries, her voice cracking as she drops it.

The dagger clatters to the floor with a metallic clang, spinning once before coming to rest against the edge of the coffee table.

For a moment, everything is still. We all stare at it, unable to tear our eyes away. The handle is carved and ornate and the blade is wickedly sharp, with serrated edges designed to tear rather than slice. The grooves well with blood, *Taylor's blood*.

She sways. Her knees buckle, and before any of us can catch her, she collapses, crumpling onto the rug. Her face lands just inches from the blade.

'Taylor!' I scream.

I fall to my knees beside her. There is blood everywhere, and it continues to flow from her hand. Howard pulls off his shirt and wraps it around the wound. The fabric turns red almost instantly.

He jerks his head up.

'Call 999!'

Clara grabs my phone and pushes it into my hand. I dial, my fingers shaking so badly I nearly drop it. My vision swims as I look from the phone to the blade lying on the floor and back again.

They put that dagger in her stocking. They wanted her to get hurt.

I press the phone to my ear. Nothing happens. I look at Howard.

'There's no coverage. Is there a house phone?'

I am walking around the room as I talk, checking all the places where you would expect to find one. Clara is right behind me.

We find a phone table in the hall. In the drawer is a phone directory, and the wall has a place for phone sockets. But there is no phone, or perhaps there was, and someone took it.

Boots. I need boots. I shove my feet into them, ignoring the laces, and stumble outside. The snow is calf deep, blocking the path and the road. I run to the gate and try my phone again. When that doesn't work, I keep trudging through the snow, the icy wind stinging my skin.

'Help!' I yell. 'Can anybody hear me?'

My voice echoes, hollow and lost, swallowed by the endless fields.

But there is no reply.

TWENTY-NINE
JOY

THE COLD CLINGS TO me like a second skin. I make it half a mile across the field before I have to turn back. My fingers and toes sting with cold, but all I can think about is Taylor. How I've failed her.

Tears stream down my face as I finally reach the cottage. My boots crunch against the threshold as I step inside. The warmth hits me, but it doesn't sink in. I'm too frozen, inside and out.

Howard looks up as I step inside, a flicker of hope breaking across his face. But it soon fades when I shake my head. His shoulders slump, and the light in his eyes dims.

'I couldn't...' The words catch in my throat.

I've failed. No signal, no help. My hands tremble as I pull off my wet gloves, useless and empty. 'I tried, but...'

Howard doesn't respond. He just nods, his gaze shifting back to our daughter.

Taylor is sprawled on the sofa, pale as the snow outside. The blood-soaked bandages on her hand stand out starkly against her skin. Howard has done his best—layers of gauze and tape wound tightly around the injury—but the stains have seeped through.

I don't think I've ever seen this much blood.

Not since the labour ward.

He's tucked a duvet around her, but it barely helps. She's trembling, teeth chattering like a wind-up toy. Her breaths come shallow and uneven, her eyes fluttering closed and open like she's fighting to stay awake.

Howard's own face is drawn, his lips pressed into a thin, grim line. I can see the worry in his eyes, the helplessness. He doesn't say anything. He doesn't need to. The silence hangs heavy between us, broken only by Taylor's shaky, laboured breaths.

I shrug off my coat, letting it fall to the floor in a damp heap, and kneel beside her. The room feels stifling and icy all at once. I reach for her face, my fingers brushing her clammy forehead. Her skin is cold—too cold.

'We need to do something! She needs help.'

But the words feel hollow. Out here, in this snow-locked nowhere, help might as well be a lifetime away.

Clara bounds across the room. She throws her arms around me.

'Mum! My doll wants to know when we can open the rest of the presents!'

Her words are innocent, cheerful, but my gaze shifts uneasily to the pile under the tree. I had completely forgotten about them. My stomach tightens. I know what was in those parcels when I placed them there, but now... after the dagger in Taylor's stocking... who knows?

'Not just yet,' I tell her.

'Oh, but Mum I want to open them!'

Clara's face twists with anger, her small fists clenched, and for a moment, I think she might stamp her foot. But then her gaze shifts to Taylor, pale and fragile on the sofa, and her expression changes. Her voice is quieter now, hesitant.

'Is Taylor going to be okay?'

'Yes,' I say, more forcefully than I intend. 'Of course she is. She just needs to rest.'

Clara bites her lip, her brow furrowing in thought. 'I don't think I like Santa anymore. That was a mean trick he played.'

I crouch down, levelling my gaze with hers. 'That wasn't Santa,' I say firmly. 'That was the Callaghans.'

She tilts her head, her frown deepening. 'But it can't have been. They don't have a key.'

My stomach tightens. She's right—they don't. I glance toward the door, as if the answer might somehow be written there.

'I know,' I admit softly, my voice laced with unease. 'It doesn't make sense to me either.'

I look at Howard. 'I couldn't find anyone out there. Are there no neighbours?'

Howard shakes his head. 'Reg said most people around here leave for the holidays. And with all this snow, even if there was someone nearby, we won't get the car through.'

But they managed it, didn't they?

There were no tracks outside, no footprints. They must have come in the night as soon as we went to sleep. And then the snow covered up their tracks. But is this the last of their nasty tricks, or do they have more up their sleeves?

Clara's squeal pierces the air as she tears into one of the presents. She holds up a Bliss doll onesie, hugging it to her chest like it's the best thing she's ever seen.

'Oh, thank you, thank you!' she cries.

I force a smile and reach for the onesie. 'Let me see that.'

I run my hands over the fabric, checking for anything unusual. My fingers linger over the seams, half expecting to find something sharp or sinister stitched into the lining. There's nothing, but I can't shake the unease crawling up my spine.

'I think we should run this through the washing machine,' I say.

Clara's face falls. 'But I want to wear it now!'

'You can wear it tonight,' I say firmly. 'It'll be ready by then.'

'We might as well open the rest,' Howard says. 'At least that way, we'll know what's in them.'

I glance at Taylor. There's nothing more I can do to help her right now. Perhaps this will take her mind off things.

We open them cautiously, inspecting each item. Howard unwraps a pair of slippers and laughs, slipping them on immediately. I feign enthusiasm for the theatre tickets he got me, but after all we've been through, the thought of sitting in a crowded auditorium makes my skin crawl.

Taylor smiles as I help her unwrap a new band t-shirt, but she's too weak to try it on.

Then Howard heads to the kitchen to make breakfast, flipping pancakes onto our plates, the syrup pooling in golden puddles. I bring a plate to Taylor and she manages to eat, but she's still deadly pale and so quiet it scares me.

Howard eats quickly, then returns to the kitchen to baste the turkey like this is any other Christmas morning. Clara chatters excitedly about the snow outside, her face pressed to the frosted windowpane.

'We always go for a Christmas walk,' she says, turning to me, her eyes bright and hopeful. 'Can we go, Mummy? Please?'

I glance at Howard, who shrugs. 'I wouldn't mind a walk. Besides, I want to get the lay of the land. And you never know, we might be able to find a phone box.'

'Okay, you take Clara. I'll stay here with Taylor.'

Clara bubbles with excitement as she bundles herself into her coat and boots.

'Be careful,' I say, my voice dropping into a warning tone. 'Don't go too far.'

'I will,' Howard promises, zipping up his jacket. 'I'll take my phone and try to get a signal. Maybe we'll run into someone else out for a walk.'

'Let's hope so,' I reply, though my words feel hollow.

I stand at the window, watching them step out into the snow. Clara skips ahead, her scarf trailing behind her. Howard follows, his eyes scanning the horizon. I glance at Taylor, still deathly pale, and back to the window.

Taylor's eyes meet mine, and she gives me a look that hurts my heart.

'Am I going to die?' she whispers, her voice trembling.

'No!'

I kneel beside her and pull her into a hug, careful not to jostle her injured hand.

'You're going to be fine,' I murmur, stroking her hair. 'I won't let anything happen to you.'

Her body is so cold that I look over at the fireplace. The fire is dwindling. I'd better build it back up again.

When I pull away, a strange expression flickers in her face, like a shadow. It catches me off guard.

'What is it?' I ask softly.

She shakes her head and looks away.

I wish I could read her mind, and decipher the thoughts behind those guarded eyes. The silence between us feels like a chasm, and I can't bridge it, no matter how desperately I want to. What is she thinking? What's she so afraid to say?

Her fingers twitch, and I catch the faintest tremor in her lip before she, shuts me out completely. I wish I could understand what she's holding onto so tightly that it's suffocating her.

THIRTY

TAYLOR

They're coming for me.

I can feel it. Somewhere out there, in that massive snow dump, they're waiting.

Watching.

Closing in.

I promised myself we'd have one last happy Christmas.

Clara deserves it. She's still at that magical age where Christmas is everything, where stockings and fairy lights are enough to make the world feel safe and whole. By next year, she won't believe in the magic anymore. By then, everything will be different.

Mum sticks *Home Alone* on for me, probably thinking it will cheer me up. I used to love this film. I'd laugh at the stupid traps and the way the villains tripped over themselves, like it was all one big joke. But now? Now it feels way too close, like some messed-up reflection of what's happening to us. Except the Callaghans aren't after our money. They're not going to screw up and get caught by the police. They're here for something worse.

I can't stop thinking about it, the way they got inside without leaving a single clue. No tracks, no sign they'd even been here, like ghosts slipping through walls.

I wonder what they will do next. I know their dad is in prison. He must know things. Little tricks of the trade. Ways of breaking into houses.

My stomach ties itself in knots, wondering what they're going to do next. I'm so weak I can barely get up off the sofa.

They could kill me while I sleep.

At least then I wouldn't have to worry about it anymore. It would all be over.
A tear trickles down my face, and I wipe it away with my good hand.

I try to concentrate on the film. I take mental notes, memorising every trap.
We could set up tripwires at the doors, scatter nails under a rug where they won't
see them. And we'll rig up something heavy to swing down and smash them in
the face. Spikes could work too, if we can find something sharp enough to draw
blood. That'll make them scream. I don't just want to stop them. I want to take
them down. And I want them to feel it.

When Clara gets back, I'll talk to her. I'm going to need her help. Right now,
I can barely move without my head spinning, but Clara? She's quick and clever,
way braver than I was at her age. She'll figure it out.

It's kind of terrifying, putting that responsibility on her, but what choice do
I have? They're coming back tonight.

I feel it in my gut.

And this time I'll be ready.

THIRTY-ONE
JOY

TAYLOR IS SITTING UP now, looking a little better, and Clara has been dashing around the house, running errands for her sister. I don't know what they're up to, but Taylor seems focused, keeping Clara busy. Maybe that's her way of distracting herself—and Clara—from everything that's happened.

Clara doesn't fully understand how dangerous things are. To her, it's still Christmas, and Christmas means fun. For the rest of us, it feels like we're holding our breath, waiting to see what comes next.

Christmas dinner isn't ready until late afternoon. Howard's always struggled with timings, and today is no exception. Eventually, we sit down to eat, but the air is heavy, every conversation forced and shallow. Clara chatters on about the snowman army she's going to build, while the rest of us concentrate on our plates.

We pull the crackers with exaggerated popping noises, laughing as Clara roars over the terrible jokes.

'My doll loves her crown,' Clara announces, adjusting the tiny paper hat on her doll's head. 'And I love my lip balm! I'm going to wear it to school and kiss all the boys.'

Howard's expression flickers with faint horror, then Clara winks, and we all dissolve into laughter. It's a strange sound. One I'd almost forgotten.

Taylor manages to eat a little, which is something, but I keep watching her, searching her face for signs of how she's really doing. There is a little more colour in her cheeks, but we still need to get her to a doctor.

At bedtime, I take Clara up to her room and read her a story, before tucking her in with her dolls. I want to ask if she's scared. If she wonders if the Callaghans will come back in the night. What they have planned for us next. The words are on the tip of my tongue, but I swallow them. She seems happy, content, untouched by the fear that's settled deep in my bones.

I smooth her hair and kiss her forehead. There's no point putting scary ideas in her head when, for now at least, she's still safe in her little bubble. I wish I climb into it with her.

I head downstairs to the lounge, ready to settle in and watch a film to keep my mind off things. The fire in the hearth has burned low, the embers glowing faintly, and the room is dim except for the soft yellow light of a lamp by the sofa. Taylor is still lying there, curled up under her duvet.

'Mum, can you turn the lights out?' she asks. 'I'm really tired.'

I hesitate, glancing towards the dark windows. 'Wouldn't you rather go up to your room?'

'I'm too tired,' she murmurs, not even opening her eyes. 'Can I sleep here for the night?'

I sigh, looking at the sofa. It's not ideal, but after what she's been through, how can I say no?

'Do you want any more paracetamol?' I ask, kneeling beside her.

'No. I feel okay,' she says softly. 'I'm just tired.'

I tuck her in just as I did Clara, minus the story and the dolls. The duvet settles around her, and for a moment, she looks peaceful. But a faint grey tinge remains in her cheeks. My mind flashes back to earlier, to all that blood dripping on the floor. I'll have to replace that rug. There's no way I'm going to get all the blood out of it. And I won't be able to get that image out of my head, either, no matter how hard I try to push it down.

I really thought we might lose her. I think it scared her too.

Upstairs, Howard is already in bed. The room is cold, despite the fact that we've got the heating on. I climb under the duvet, but my mind refuses to settle. Howard sets his phone down on the nightstand and turns to me.

'What if they smash the windows? Taylor could get covered in glass.'

I shake my head. 'They don't need to. They got in last night without breaking anything. I still can't understand how they did it.'

There's no neighbour here they could've tricked out of a spare key. No easy explanation.

'Could they have arrived before us?' Howard says after a pause. 'The keys were easy to find if you knew where to look. And there was only one set under the stone when we arrived, but what if there had been a second set? They could have taken them without us knowing.'

I frown, turning onto my side to face him. 'How could they possibly know where we were going?'

He picks up his phone again. The screen's glow illuminates his furrowed brow.

'Reg sent me the instructions for the cottage. What if they've found some way of getting into my emails?'

The thought sends a chill down my spine. 'Can they do that?'

'They broke into our house, didn't they? So it follows that they might have looked at the computer.'

I groan as I think of the big yellow password taped to the monitor.

What were we thinking?

We lie there in the darkness, the faint creaks of the old house settling around us.

'What if they come back tonight, while we're all asleep?'

'This time, I'll be ready for them.'

He has a strange look in his eye. A steely determination that sends a shiver down my back.

'What are you planning to do?'

He glances around, as if he's afraid someone might be listening, and when he speaks, his voice is low and deliberate:

'I'm going to give it a couple of hours. Let them think we're all asleep, then I'm going to hide out in the woodshed.'

'But what if they show up? Then what will you do?'

He leans under the bed. I draw back as he holds up an enormous axe. The blade curves slightly, a vicious arc that looks as though it could bite deep with the slightest swing.

'What...what are you going to do with that?'

He doesn't meet my eye. 'Whatever I have to.'

THIRTY-TWO
TAYLOR

I SIT BY THE window, watching the snow fall in silence. The house feels still, heavy with the quiet of the night. Mum, Dad, and Clara should be asleep by now, but my brain won't shut up. It keeps spinning, going over everything. Clara's done well. She followed my instructions perfectly, setting up everything exactly how I asked.

Out in the garden, there's the pit she dug. It's not huge—she only had the little spade from the shed—but it's deep enough to trip them up. She covered it with an old white blanket so it just looks like snow. It won't trap them, not really, but it might slow them down or make them fall.

Closer to the house, I had her set up the cans. They're scattered right in front of the door, ready to rattle and clang if someone kicks them. It'll make enough noise to wake everyone—or at least, that's the plan.

If they still make it through the door, there's the bucket. I balanced it on the shelf. It took ages to get it set up, but now it's positioned just right. The second they walk in, it'll tip, soaking them with freezing cold water.

Then there are the drawing pins. I scattered an entire box of them by the front and back doors. They're small, but those sharp little points are hard to spot. If they step on them, they'll feel it, even through their shoes. Hopefully, they'll make a lot of noise too, yelling and screaming in pain.

I promised myself I'd stay awake until morning. I want to keep watch, just in case. That's why I chose to sleep down here. I've got my backpack next to me, with the hammer inside. If anyone makes it into the house, I'll be ready for them.

I'm normally great at staying awake, but tonight my body has other ideas. I feel so weak and my head feels so heavy, that each blink lasts longer than the last.

Just a minute, I tell myself as I lie back against the pillows. I just need a brief rest. My eyelids flutter, and before I can stop it, the room fades into black.

THIRTY-THREE
JOY

MY EYES FLICK TO the axe in my husband's hands. It looks heavy. The thought of him actually swinging it at someone feels surreal.

'What are you going to do with that? You're not... you wouldn't actually...'

'I don't know,' he admits quietly, his grip tightening on the handle. 'But I'll be ready. At the very least, I can scare them off.'

I study his face, searching for something—hesitation, fear, a crack in his resolve—but there's nothing. Just grim determination.

I want to believe he can do it, that he's capable of chasing the Callaghans away, of keeping us safe.

They don't know him like I do. If he looks tough enough, if he stands his ground, maybe it'll be enough to scare them off.

'Just... be careful.' My eyes dart to the clock on the wall. The second hand ticks forward.

'In a couple of hours, it'll be midnight. You should go down to the woodshed at quarter to. Then you'll be ready. It will be cold out there, so make sure you wear plenty of layers. I don't want you to catch your death.'

He nods grimly, and that's it.

It's decided.

The house falls silent. It's the kind of silence that presses against your ears so you invent noises that are not real. Like when you hold a shell to your ear and fancy you can hear the sea. It's a delusion. A sleight of nature's hand. But it's enough to keep me on my toes.

Neither of us sleep. We lie there, staring in turn at the ceiling, the clock, and the window. And we whisper to each other. Hushed fragments of conversation to fill the void. We used to do this, when we were first together, but back then it was excitement that kept me awake. The giddiness of first love. Now it is trepidation. The knowledge of what must be done.

By a quarter to midnight, Howard is already up and dressed. He slips quietly down the stairs; the axe gripped tightly in one hand, his other steadying himself on the banister. I follow as far as the landing, and sit on the top stair while he gets ready. The night air has teeth and I wrap my dressing gown more tightly around me, wishing that my heart wouldn't hammer so loud.

He reaches for his boots, then lets out a yelp.

I rush down the stairs. 'What's wrong?'

He plucks a drawing pin from the sole of his sock, holding it up to the light. His lips press into a thin line as he places it on the table. I notice more pins on the floor and I point them out. He picks them all up, shaking his head as he creates a small pile. Then he pulls on his boots, straightens up, and opens the door.

Before he can step outside, a bucket teeters on the high shelf and crashes down, drenching him with water. He lets out a sharp gasp, stumbling backward as the icy shock sends him reeling. His foot slips on the slick, wet floor, and he loses his balance.

With a dull thud, the back of his head connects with the banister, and he groans, water dripping from his hair and soaking into his clothes. He sits there for a moment, dazed, shaking droplets off his face like a dog caught in the rain.

'Dad!' Taylor's voice cuts through the quiet as she rushes in from the lounge, her face pale. 'Oh, Dad! That wasn't meant for you! That was for the Callaghans.'

Howard lets out a laugh. 'You got me!' he says, rubbing the back of his head.

Taylor lingers in the doorway. 'I didn't think you'd... I mean, I didn't know you'd be going out at this time of night.'

'It's okay,' he says, waving a hand dismissively. 'But maybe next time... warn us first?'

I grab a towel from the kitchen and hand it to him. 'Come on, Howard. Let's get you dry before you catch pneumonia.'

He sighs heavily, his breath fogging slightly in the cold air. 'Well, so much for the element of surprise.'

Howard sits in the kitchen while I make him a hot cocoa.

'My head is banging,' he admits, once Taylor has gone back to bed.

'I don't think you're in a fit state to take on the Callaghans,' I say, setting the mug down in front of him.

'But what if they turn up?'

'I'll go,' I say impulsively. 'Same plan, but I'm the one who'll go to the woodshed. You'll stay in the house with the girls.'

He frowns deeply. 'I don't know, Joy...'

'Why not?' I challenge him. 'What difference does it make if it's me instead of you?'

He bites his tongue. I know he doesn't like it, but my mind is made up. Quickly, I shove on my coat and boots, picking up another stray pin as I do. I pick up the axe and head outside.

I stand on the porch for a moment and listen to the silence. If the Callaghans come tonight, they'll have to be on foot. There's no way a car is getting through these roads. In fact, I can only imagine they are sleeping in their car too. Unless they've broken into an empty holiday cottage. I wouldn't put it past them.

I make my way towards the woodshed, my breath clouding in the freezing night air. The garden is eerily quiet except for the crunch of my boots on the snow. I step carefully around the big ditch Clara dug in the middle of the yard, my eyes scanning the darkness.

The door of the woodshed creaks as I pull it open and check there's no one inside. It crosses my mind too late that this could be where they are hiding, and that I'm just about to step into an ambush. Thankfully, there is nothing inside but piles of wood.

The air smells damp and earthy, with a faint metallic tang from the old tools hanging on the walls. My breath fogs in the air, and I focus on keeping it quiet, steady, though my chest feels tight with nerves.

The axe feels heavy in my hands, its wooden handle rough against my palm. I shift slightly and a shiver runs through me, but it's not just the cold—it's the waiting, the not knowing.

A faint tickle brushes my cheek. I flinch and swipe at it. My hand comes away with a strand of web, almost invisible in the faint light seeping through the gap in the door. I squint into the darkness. I imagine spiders, large and leggy, lurking in the corners, their webs draped across the beams like veils. My phone is in my pocket. If I wanted, I could pull it out and use it as a torch. But I don't want to see them. It's bad enough to imagine.

I keep the door open just enough to watch the garden. I listen to the rustle of the branches and the rattle of the roof in the wind. And I grip the axe tighter, using fear to keep me focused. The spiders don't matter. The cold doesn't matter. All that matters is my family.

I look down at the axe, at its sharp glinting blade.

Earlier, I asked Howard if he thought he use it, if he had to.

Now I know I can.

THIRTY-FOUR
JOY

FOOTSTEPS CRUNCH THROUGH THE snow. They move like an army, not quite in formation, but definitely organised, as if they have practised. This isn't just a game to them. They've planned this. They've prepared.

I press tighter into the shadows, straining to hear them over the pounding of my heart. Their voices come in short, low bursts, carried on the cold night air.

'You sure they'll be asleep?' one of them says, her tone sharp, impatient.

'I would think so by now.'

'I wouldn't be, if it were me. I wouldn't sleep a wink.'

I don't hear what's said next, but there's a burst of laughter. The sound is jarring, like a piano being hurled downstairs. It tumbles through the cold night air, shattering the stillness and leaving an uneasy echo in its wake.

'Shut up, all of you! Do you want them to know we're coming?'

'What are they going to do, anyway?'

Their voices are quiet after that. I barely catch a word as the gate creaks open. They're in the garden now.

'Hey, watch your feet, Angel.'

Angel. Which one is that?

I ease the door open a little further to get a better look. Six girls as always, paired off in neat little twos. The tallest ones leading, smallest trailing behind. The little ones have their heads down, hands shoved deep into their coat pockets. They move slower than the rest, their steps less certain. One of them keeps glancing back at the road, her shoulders hunched like she's hoping for some excuse to turn around. She knows she shouldn't be here. Perhaps she has a conscience.

I feel a well of anger at seeing those young ones out here like this. They should be tucked up in bed, not being led on a crazy night time mission to attack my family. They don't belong.

But they're here all the same, following orders, letting themselves be dragged into something dangerous. I focus my anger on the two tallest ones. And on myself, for not stopping this sooner.

I tighten my grip on the axe.

I'm ready.

I'm going to put the fear of god into them, and if someone gets hurt, so be it.

They are just a couple of metres from the cottage when the tallest one turns to face them, her posture stiff. Her gaze flicks over the others, as if she's inspecting her troops.

'Right.' Her tone is sharp, decisive. 'Let's finish this.'

She turns and walks on. I hold my breath as she approaches Clara's ditch, completely unaware of what lies beneath the thin blanket of snow. Her boots crunch against the frosty ground. She doesn't even glance down. The moment her foot hits the hidden edge of the pit, it sinks, throwing her off balance. She stumbles forward, her arms shooting out for support. The second girl follows too closely, her foot slipping into the same spot.

'Careful!' one of them snaps, grabbing onto the nearest arm to steady herself. The group slows, their movements jerky as they struggle to regain their footing. The smallest one wobbles precariously, her arms flailing as the others shift around her, but someone pulls her upright.

They look at each other, muttering something too low for me to catch, but none of them stop to investigate. They brush it off, probably assuming it's just uneven ground under the snow.

I step out from the shadows, gripping the axe tightly in both hands. My breath fogs the icy air, and the world feels smaller, the snow muffling everything but their voices.

Their backs are to me. I watch as the eldest one feels in her pocket and produces a key.

I close the distance between us in an instant, careful to walk around the ditch.

One of them swings round to look at me.

'What...'

I swing the axe, the blade arcing through the air and slamming into the ground just inches from their feet. The snow sprays, and they jump back, stumbling over each other.

'Get away from us!' I yell, the sound ripping from my throat, more animal than human.

Their eyes go wide, fear flashing across their faces, but it doesn't stop them. The tallest one lunges for me, her hands reaching for the axe. I yank it back, twisting sharply to keep her off, but the younger one, small and wiry runs behind me and leaps onto my back like a wildcat, her hands wrapping around my neck, almost knocking me off balance.

'Get it!' she screams.

Her hands are still round my neck. She's squeezes with both hands, making me cough and splutter.

I stagger forward, my boots skidding on the slick snow. I hear the blood rushing in my ears. Her breath is hot against my ears. I try to pull off her fingers with one hand, but I can't let go of the axe. The other girls try to wrench it from my hands.

'Let go!' the tallest one barks, yanking hard.

I tighten my grip, digging my heels into the ground. Then I bend forward without warning and she comes flying off, right over my shoulder onto the ground. I hope that hurt.

I suck down air.

The tallest girl doesn't back off. We both have our hands on axe, but I'm the one in control. I swing it wildly, not caring who gets hurt. I must have cut her because she shrieks and jumps away. I hold it over my head triumphantly. Glaring around the group to show them I mean business.

I roar, my voice shaking with fury.

The youngest is still lying on the ground. She looks up at me with such hate that it shocks me. One of her sisters hauls her to her feet.

I point the blade at her, and she takes a big step back.

'Enough!' the tallest one snaps, grabbing her by the arm. 'Let's go.'

They retreat, slipping and sliding in the snow, disappearing back into the dark. They leave the gate hanging. I follow them a little way to see where they go. I see the lights of their torches bobbing in the distance. They head down the lane and cross the field. Their car must be some way off.

What lengths they've gone to on this cold night just to torment us. I clutch the axe tightly in my hand and turn back towards the cottage.

The garden is silent again, the snow glistening in the moonlight, but my ears are still ringing, my pulse throbbing in my throat. I glance down at the blade, now streaked with dirt and snow. My arms ache, but I don't let go.

I walk towards the door, but when I reach it, I spot something shiny poking out of the snow. I bend down and pick it up, and my heart leaps out of my chest.

The key! I made them drop their key.

I punch the air, unable to believe my good fortune.

I've won for now, but I know this isn't over. The Callaghans don't give up so easily.

Tomorrow, they'll be back.

THIRTY-FIVE
TAYLOR

MUM COMES INTO THE house, still gripping the axe. Her cheeks are flushed from the cold. Her eyes wide. I can't believe she did that. She took on the Callaghans—*actually* took them on—and won.

That was... incredible.

She sets the axe down against the wall, her hand lingering on it for a second before she turns to lock the door behind her.

'Better put that away. We don't want Clara picking it up,' Dad says.

'Let's take it up to bed with us. I feel safer knowing I have it to hand.'

They glance in on me, and I shrink down under the duvet, pretending to be asleep. I listen as they head up the stairs and I take another look outside.

All clear. But I'm not taking anything for granted. So I sit by the window, resting my chin on my knees. I'll stay awake for a few more hours, in case. Like all old people, my parents wake early in the morning. I just need to keep watch until they do.

I switch on the TV but keep the volume down low. There's nothing on except weird chat shows and old people films, but I watch anyway. I stay awake until six in the morning, when I hear my family moving around. Only then do I let my guard down. Sleep hits me like a brick, and I'm instantly swept into a strange, restless sleep.

In the dream, I'm one of Clara's dolls. I can't move on my own; she's the one in control, dragging me around and making me do whatever she wants. I try to speak, to stop her, but my mouth won't open. It's like being trapped in my own body.

When I wake up, the dream stays with me. I shake it off. My mouth is as dry as old toast and my throat aches like I've been on the phone with Aunt Dorothy all night. I stumble out of bed and head to the kitchen, grabbing a Coke from the fridge. I enjoy the spray of fizz as I pop it open and drink it down in one go.

As I head into the hallway, something catches my eye. One of Clara's dolls lies face down on the floor, its little dress crumpled, one arm bent at an unnatural angle. I crouch down and pick it up, turning it over in my hands. Its painted eyes stare blankly back at me, unblinking. How does Clara not find this creepy?

I head upstairs with it. I'm still a little weak, so I have to stop at the top and get my breath back. I knock on Clara's door, but she doesn't reply. I push it open and glance inside. Her bed is empty, the covers thrown back in a heap. I toss the doll onto her bed, watching as it bounces once before settling awkwardly on the pillow.

Mum bursts into the room, her eyes wide and frantic. 'Clar...Oh, it's you.'

'Yeah, it's me.'

Mum blinks. She looks at me weirdly, like she's expecting me to explain something.

'Where's Clara?'

I shrug. 'Probably in the loo.'

'No, she isn't.' Her eyes dart around the room and the unease creeps up into my chest.

'She's not downstairs or in the garden,' Dad says, appearing in the doorway.

'Did you try the woodshed?'

'I tried everywhere.'

The three of us look at each other, the realisation hitting us all at once.

She's gone.

THIRTY-SIX
JOY

I don't even remember screaming, but my throat feels raw and my ears ring with the echo of my own voice. The room is spinning, a blur of Howard pacing, Taylor bolting for the door.

There is a sick weight crushing my chest.

Howard tries to stay calm. His voice is measured as he fumbles with his phone. He keeps redialling 999 and staring at the screen like sheer willpower might make it work. But the signal's dead, the same as yesterday. There's no Wi-Fi, nothing. Just the silence of this godforsaken place.

I have to find her.

I drag myself downstairs. Taylor flings the front door open and runs out into the snow. For a moment, all I can do is stand there, watching her dark shape against the white. Then I throw on my coat and boots and stagger out after her.

Footprints.

She's following footprints, faint and uneven in the snow. My breath comes in sharp, painful bursts as I try to catch up. The prints lead out into the road, then curve right, toward the main track we drove in on when we arrived.

That's where they stop.

'Clara…' The name comes out as a whisper, barely audible over the wind. My legs threaten to give way, but I force myself to keep going.

How did they get in? My mind races, grasping for logic, but it slips through my fingers like water. Both doors were locked last night. I double-checked. And I have their key. I fumble in my pocket. Yes, I still have it. So how…

The back door! They must have a key for that too. How could I be so stupid?

Pressure builds in my skull, a relentless pounding that drowns out everything else. My legs barely hold me as I stumble after Taylor.

'Help!' The word tears from my throat, hoarse and desperate. 'Please! Someone, help us!'

The mountains throw the sound back at me, a hollow echo that only makes the silence worse. A bird flutters out of a nearby tree, startled, then the world settles into stillness again.

Howard is at the door now, pulling on his coat.

'There must be someone out there,' he says. 'A farmer. A hiker. Anyone.'

I grab his hand and squeeze it. My grip is weak, but I can't let go. 'Hurry,' I whisper.

He nods and disappears after Taylor into the snow.

They walk across the fields and, to my shame; I head back to the house.

There could be a ransom note, I reason. What if this has just been about money, all along?

I wish I could believe that but I know it's unlikely.

I thought I was tough, but this is more than I can take. I barely make it back indoors before I collapse onto the floor.

My heart feels like it's swelling, stretching against my ribs. Clara's name reverberates through me, filling every corner of my being. I curl up there on the carpet, unable to get up, my back against the cold wall.

The house is too quiet. No washing machine running, no muffled chatter from the next room. Just the silence of snow pressing in on all sides.

'Clara!' I whisper into the void, clutching my knees to my chest. My ears strain for the faintest sound, for any sign of her. I want so badly to believe in something—some unspoken connection that would let me feel her presence. But there's nothing.

Tears spill over, hot against my freezing skin.

A new thought strikes me like a blow:

What if she's already dead?

The room spins, my breath coming in sharp, shallow bursts. I pitch forward onto my hands and knees, dry heaving as the weight of it threatens to crush me.

I crawl into the kitchen and rummage through the first aid box, knocking over a bottle of iodine and scattering plasters across the counter. The paracetamol rattle against my teeth as I pop two into my mouth, chasing them down with a gulp of water. The chalky bitterness clings to the back of my throat, leaving a taste like stale paper and metal on my tongue.

Somewhere in the distance, I hear a sound. Is that Clara's voice? Taylor's?

I drag myself back down the hall, gripping the edge of the doorframe as I peer outside. The garden is empty, but the snow is disturbed, criss-crossed with footprints. My own prints. Taylor's. Howard's. It's hard to distinguish one set from another.

'Clara!'

A part of me still thinks she's hiding in the woodshed, or something, and any minute she's going to jump out and surprise me.

'Clara!'

Then I see it.

On the doormat, half-buried in the snow, lies something small. I stoop down and pick it up, my hands trembling as I recognise the painted face. Clara's doll. The new one.

I stare at it, my chest tightening. Its head lolls to one side, and as I lift it, it falls off completely, landing in the snow with a *plop*.

The head stares up at me and I scream loud enough to shake the snow from the branches of the surrounding trees.

Is this what they've done with my daughter?

THIRTY-SEVEN

TAYLOR

MY NOSE IS SO cold it feels like I've been snorting razor blades. I hurry to keep up with Dad, but it's like wading through cement. He hasn't said a word about how slow I'm going, but I can feel his frustration. He's walking ahead, his jaw tight, eyes scanning the horizon. Every so often we stop to shout, just in case she can hear us:

'Clara!'

My guts tie themselves in knots, cramping and twisting as I picture her with them. What are they doing to her?

If only I hadn't...

I shake my head, pushing the thought away. There's no time for this. I glance at Dad. His steady stride is the only thing keeping me sane. He doesn't say it, but I know he blames himself too. Maybe that's why neither of us can look at each other.

'What's the plan?' I ask, breaking the silence.

'We keep following the tracks.'

We push forward. My arm throbs with every movement, but I grit my teeth and keep going.

Then something moves in the distance.

'What's that?' I ask, squinting.

Dad stops, his eyes narrowing. A small creature bounds through the snow, brown fur flashing against the icy landscape.

'Just a dog,' he says.

I watch it for a moment. The scruffy terrier's movements seem familiar. And then it clicks.

'It's their dog,' I whisper.

Dad glances at me. 'The Callaghans?'

I nod, my chest tightening. 'That's Kingsley.'

The terrier sniffs the ground, then looks up at us. He freezes for a second, ears perked, and then bolts toward the river.

'What's he doing out on his own?' Dad says.

'Maybe he's lost.'

'Maybe he could lead us to Clara.'

We both pick up the pace, following the dog as fast as we can. My legs feel like lead, and my breath comes in short, sharp bursts, but I force myself to keep up.

When we reach the riverbank, my stomach lurches.

'Kingsley! Here boy! Stop. Stop!'

Kingsley bounds ahead, jumping onto the ice. His small paws skid and he barks frantically. He runs in circles, slipping with every step.

Dad finds a stick on the riverbank and holds it out to him, but the dog takes no notice. He doesn't seem to understand we want to save him. He just keeps skidding around. Dad moves closer.

'Come on, here, boy!'

He's still not close enough. He puts one foot on the ice.

'Don't go any closer,' I say, grabbing his arm.

'We can't just leave him,' Dad says. 'Come on, boy.'

He takes another step.

'Dad, no!' I cry, panic rising.

He extends the stick toward the dog again.

'Grab it!' he urges.

Kingsley scrambles forward, his claws scratching uselessly at the ice. Finally, he lays eyes on the stick. One ear lifts. Dad wobbles precariously while he sniffs it like a treat. Then he clamps his teeth around it.

'That's it, hold on tight,' Dad says, his voice steady despite the cracks spider webbing beneath him.

I edge closer, ready to pull him back if the ice gives way.

'Dad, come back now!'

Slowly, he steps back, dragging Kingsley inch by inch toward the bank. The ice groans under his weight, and then, with a loud crack, his foot plunges through it.

'Dad!' I lunge forward, grabbing his arm as the whole sheet gives way.

He grabs onto me, and hauls himself and the dog back onto the bank, where we collapse in a heap. Kingsley stands there, barking furiously as if this was all our fault.

'You have to go back and change,' I tell Dad. 'You'll freeze.'

'I need to find Clara!'

'I'll go.'

'No, not on your own. Let's both go back. I'll get dried off and you can find something to tie to him. That way, he won't run off again.'

I nod, and lift the Kingsley into my arms. I'm not letting him out of my sight again. Not until he leads us to Clara.

THIRTY-EIGHT
CLARA

Two hours earlier

I SHAKE STAR. HER eyelashes flutter open. I peer over the edge of the bed and look at the other dolls.

'Are you awake?' I whisper. Nobody responds. I pick them all up and sit them on the bed. Then I give them tea. I pour myself a cup and take a sip, remembering to stick out my pinkie finger, the proper way.

After we've all finished, I pour the water back into the teapot and help the dolls into my backpack one by one.

I slip out of bed and out into the corridor. Dad's snores echo around the landing like an earthquake. I grab the pillow from my bed and place it at the top of the stairs, then I ride it: bump, bump, bump, all the way to the bottom.

I get to my feet and head into the kitchen to check for rats. I really like rats. I wish Mum and Dad had let us keep them. It's so unfair. All my friends have pets, even Bess. She's got an orange gerbil. His name is Kevin.

There are no animals in the kitchen, but we do have biscuits. I take three. There are crisps in the cupboard as well. I take a packet and pop it into my backpack in case the dolls get hungry. Then I wander into the living room. Taylor is lying on the sofa. I stand there for a moment, spying on her. She doesn't look very comfortable, with her legs hanging over the edge like that. Emily thinks I should tickle her toes, but I tell her no.

Sometimes Taylor is my friend, and other times she's an enemy. Mum says it's because she's a teenager, and teenagers have hormones. I have hormones too, but not as many as Taylor. I'm going to get more of them when I get older. I'm going to get more teeth too. I check my wobbly one to see if it's still there. It's really loose now but I'm a bit disappointed it didn't fall out on Christmas Day. That would have been fun. Even Taylor thought so.

I rummage through my bag and pull out Tiffany. I place her in the corridor to guard Taylor while she sleeps.

I am so bored. I go to the window and look outside. It has snowed even more. Lovely fresh snow that begs to be stomped on. I throw on my coat and shoes and turn the key ever so quietly so I don't wake anyone. For a moment I just stand in the doorway, looking at it all. It never snows this much in London. I wish I had a phone, so I could take some pictures. Even Bess has her own phone. I hope Taylor gets a new one for her birthday, then I can have hers.

I remember my backpack and put it on before I hop down the steps. I look around, wondering what to do first. Should I build a snowman or an igloo?

I decide on a snowman. I've never built a real one before. We never get enough snow. Usually. Taylor and I scrape as much as we can off the car. Last year I took some off the plant pots, but Mum said I should leave it to keep them warm. The windowsills are always good though. Lots of snow there.

It is unbelievably snowy. I could probably build a whole family of snowmen. The dolls all think it's a great idea, so I set to work, rolling snow into a ball. The ball gets heavier and heavier until I reach the bottom of the garden. I gaze at it with satisfaction. This one can be the daddy snowman, since it's so big. Perhaps I can borrow Daddy's glasses to help it see? As I bend down to gather more snow for his body, I hear a faint rumbling sound, like a car engine. I look up, but I can't see a car. Maybe it's a snow plough. Daddy told me they all have funny names in Scotland, like Sled Zepelin and Mr Andy Flurry. He has an app on his phone so we can see where they all are. It makes him smile.

I start on Daddy snowman's body. I push it along, pressing it tighter and tighter. My fingers are numb, but I don't care. The snow is just right. It's going to be perfect.

The shadow falls over me so slowly I don't even notice at first. Then, out of nowhere, a hand clamps down on my face. My eyes sting as tears well up, hot and fast. I try to scream, but the sound is swallowed by the hand.

I kick and wriggle as I'm lifted off the ground. My snowball keeps rolling and my heart beats faster than it ever has before.

'Got her? Good. Did anybody see?'

Their voices are sharp and low, like hissing snakes. I try to yell again, but my tongue feels too big for my mouth. Then they shove something in—something scratchy and rough—pressing it against my teeth.

It feels like a sock.

I gag, but they don't stop. My nose feels like it's closing up, and I can't get enough air. I wriggle my arms and legs, but I can't get away.

They pass me between them like a rugby ball. Their hands are rough and careless, like I'm not even a person. I kick my legs as hard as I can, but then a sharp slap cracks across my cheek, and it burns like fire.

I try to breathe through my nose, sucking in cold air, but it's not enough. My head feels floaty, my chest too tight, like it's going to pop.

I can't stop crying. The tears blur everything—the trees, the ground, the snow. I see branches flashing past and reach out, clawing at them. My fingers scrape bark, but it slips away.

I twist my head, looking back, straining to see the gate. I want to go back. Back to the garden. Back to my family.

But it's too far now.

My chest heaves, and my face feels wet and sticky with snot and tears. My brain is screaming, but I can't get the words out.

I want my Mummy. I want her so badly it hurts.

THIRTY-NINE
JOY

I STARE AT THE decapitated doll.

I've always found Clara's dolls a little freaky. I've only pretended to like them because Clara is so crazy about them. This one looks up at me, its eyes vacant, yet somehow vaguely human.

I grab my coat from inside, along with the keys and head out to the car. I shift the bulk of the snow off the roof, then get the door open so I can lean in and switch on the engine. Hopefully, it will do most of the work, defrosting the front and back windows.

While that's going on, I go into the woodshed to look for a shovel. I can't find it, so I pick up a thick bristled broom. I suppose that will have to do. I get to work, sweeping a path up the driveway. I'm sweating in my ski jacket, but I keep working, knowing every minute counts. I imagine Clara is standing next to me, hands on hips.

Missed a bit.

I sweep until I reach the road. There were no tyre tracks up here, so they must have taken her on foot. But unless they've got a tractor or a tank, they're not going to get very far in this weather.

I return to the car. The snow has melted from the windows. I finish it off with a towel and then get behind the wheel. I need to turn the car around, but the driveway is so snowy I'm not sure how I'm going to do it.

With a quick flick of the wheel, I manoeuvre onto the lane and start down the driveway. The tyres struggle against the snowy terrain, but I keep my cool and maintain control. After all, haven't I driven through much more treacherous conditions?

This should be a piece of cake.

As I continue down the unfamiliar road, doubts creep in. Which way did they take her? Where could she be now? My gaze sweeps over the passing scenery, desperately searching for any sign of civilization. But all I see are endless fields and towering trees, their branches weighed down by snow.

All at once, there is a loud groan from beneath me and I feel resistance. The wheels spin, sending a spray of snow onto the windshield and now the car's stop moving.

Damn!

I slam my hands against the steering wheel, hitting the horn. The blaring noise shatters the silence, blaring out over the snow-covered fields. If there's anyone out there—locals, holidaymakers, anyone—they ought to hear. Someone might be close enough to help, to stumble across us or come looking to see what the commotion is.

I lean into it, letting the sound carry into the air.

I wait for a minute, but there is no response. Then I slide out of the car and start walking.

'Help!' I yell. 'Can anybody hear me? I need your help!'

I stop and listen, but the surrounding countryside is eerily still. It's as if everyone's left for the winter, but I know that can't be true. There must be someone left.

Oh Clara!

I still can't believe this is happening. None of it feels real. I brush the tears from my eyes and push myself forward, trudging onwards until I see an odd shape at the side of the road.

What is that?

I scrape off the snow to reveal heavy duty yellow plastic. It's a grit bin. I ease open the lid and look down at the contents. If I remember rightly, they fill them with a combination of grit and salt. I take great handfuls of it and make a huge heap on the ground, then I set to work, sprinkling the road. The snow sparkles in the sunlight, and I cross my fingers that the salt will help it dissolve. I unzip my coat and hold out my shirt in front of me, so that I can fill the front of it with grit.

The walk back seems longer. I skid and slide as I scatter the salt and grit. I don't know if it's really helping or if I'm just kidding myself. But at least this way I feel like I'm doing something.

The lane stretches ahead of me, a narrow ribbon swallowed by the snow. I crunch the snow beneath my feet. The sound reminds me of Clara biting into an apple.

Her name is a drumbeat in my mind, loud and relentless.

What have they done to you?
What are they going to do?

My lungs feel as though they've shrunk. The question claws at me, the images too horrific to push away. I picture Clara frightened, her small hands trembling. I imagine her calling out for me, her voice breaking, and a fresh wave of nausea rolls over me.

'Clara!' I shout, my voice hoarse and desperate.

Nothing answers. Not the wind, not a distant voice, not even the sound of another footstep.

I stumble onward, my legs aching from the thick snow, my eyes scanning the road ahead. And then, I see it.

A splash of red in the whiteness.

I run towards it, my breath hitching. My pulse races as I get closer.

It's Emily.

Clara's doll lies on her side in the snow, her red dress vivid against the endless white.

My knees buckle as I crouch down and reach for her, brushing the wetness from her plastic body. She is not frosty, not yet. She hasn't been out here long enough. Her serene face stares back at me and I search her for clues. She's lost her shoes. She had little glass slippers like Cinderella. If I keep walking, will I find them too? Someone has left this doll like a breadcrumb for me to find.

But was it Clara, or the Callaghans?

Are they toying with me, daring me to follow?

Or has Clara left me a clue? My clever, precocious child.

I tighten my grip on the doll, tears stinging my eyes as I stand. The snow swirls around me, the world spinning. I look down the empty road. The trees blur together in the distance.

I tuck Emily into my coat pocket. Her hard plastic limbs press against me as I force my feet to move. The cold eats at my fingers. Then I hear a bark and I turn to look at the fields. I spot two people walking over the fields towards me.

It's Howard and Taylor, and trotting along beside them, is a bedraggled dog.

'Did you get help?'

Howard shakes his head. 'No, but we found their dog.'

I look at the terrier. It does look sort of familiar. But all dogs look the same to me.

'How do you know it's their dog?'

He's got his name on his collar. 'Kingsley Callaghan.'

Kingsley trots up to me, then circles back to Taylor, tail wagging. She doesn't look at me, her hood is pulled low over her face. I wonder what she's thinking, but the wind pushes me forward before I can dwell on it.

'I rescued him from the river.' Howard says. 'I need to get back and dry off.'

'Do you think they'll swap Kingsley for Clara?'

'It's possible, but we don't have a way of reaching them. We're going head back and get some string to tie to his collar. Then maybe he'll lead us to them.'

I want to answer. At least he has a plan, but I can't say anything. The tears are flowing again. I can't make them stop. To my surprise, Taylor wraps her arms around me. My good, kind girl.

'It's like a physical pain,' I finally say. 'It hurts so much.'

'I know,' Taylor says.

Howard nods, his teeth chattering too hard. We walk together towards the car. Taylor has her phone out as she desperately tries to get a signal. She keeps glancing at the screen, shaking it in frustration.

When we reach the car, Howard and Taylor climb in, while I scrape away the snow clinging stubbornly to the tires. My fingers burn from the cold as I rub the last of the salt over them, hoping it'll be enough. I climb into the driver's seat, my heart thudding as I turn the key. Relief floods through me as the engine roars to life, steady and smooth. The sound is soothing, like a cat's purr.

I reverse carefully; the car skidding and sliding over the icy ground, my hands gripping the wheel tightly. As soon as I park, Howard and Taylor jump out and hurry towards the house.

Howard opens the door. I didn't even think to lock it. After all, what else do I have to lose?

He bends down and picks something up from the welcome mat. He stares at it, then looks at Taylor. The expression in his eyes is somewhere between shock and fear. Taylor freezes, her hand hovering near her phone.

I slam the car door and run toward them, the icy ground crunching beneath my boots.

'What is it?'

Howard hands it to me: a blank postcard with uneven, jagged letters scrawled in red. They look like claw marks, red and angry.

I hold it up to the light and read:

TIME TO FESS UP, TAYLOR. OR YOU'LL HAVE MORE BLOOD ON YOUR HANDS.

FORTY

JOY

I HAVE NO IDEA what the note refers to, but I've felt it all along, this nagging feeling that there has to be a reason for all this. Why the Callaghans have targeted us. It all started with Taylor. When they followed her home from the shopping centre. They didn't bother Lucy, even though they clearly know where she lives.

I look at Taylor now.

'What is it you aren't telling us?'

She shakes her head, but she can't look me in the eye.

Howard places a warning hand on my shoulder, but I shake him off.

I look at my daughter, at the dark rings around her eyes. I thought she was just stressed, same as we were.

'How did you know it was their dog, Taylor?'

She looks at me. 'It says on his collar.'

I look at Howard. 'You knew before we looked at the collar,' he says softly.

I wait a beat. Two. The silence stretches, heavier than the cold air around us, but still, Taylor doesn't speak.

Howard shifts uneasily beside me, breaking the tension. 'I think we should talk about this inside,' he says quietly, his voice calm but firm.

Before I can respond, Taylor pushes past us. The door slams behind her, rattling in its frame.

Howard exhales sharply. 'I'll go,' he says, reaching for the doorknob.

I reach out and stop him, shaking my head. 'No. You need to take a shower and get warm.'

'This is more important,' he argues, his voice tight with frustration.

'You won't be much use to Clara if you catch pneumonia.'

He hesitates, his lips pressing into a thin line. 'Fine. I'll be as quick as I can.'

As he heads to the bathroom, I follow him up the stairs. When I reach the landing, I sink down onto the carpet, leaning against the wall outside Taylor's room.

I hear her crying through the wall. The sound cuts through me. I sit there for a moment, staring at the closed door, unsure what to do. My instincts scream at me to barge in and demand answers, but if I push too hard, she might clam up again.

Instead, I take a deep breath and call softly, 'I'm just out here, when you're ready to talk.'

There's no reply.

I press my palms against my knees, forcing myself to stay calm. 'Please,' I say. My voice trembles despite my efforts to keep it steady. 'We need to know everything. It's the only way we can help Clara.'

The silence stretches again, broken only by her quiet, shuddering sobs. I lean my head back against the wall. Time feels like it's slipping through my fingers. I shut my eyes, and when I open them, Howard emerges from the bathroom, dressed in a fresh jumper and joggers.

'Taylor?' he says, knocking on the door. 'It's Dad. I'm coming in.'

FORTY-ONE
TAYLOR

Three Months Earlier

STAR TAKES A SIP of her tea and sets it down on the nightstand. Her eyes look a bit puffy and she's barely looked at me since I arrived. She seems obsessed with a paint splotch on the wall. It's not like it's a new stain. It's been there at least half a year.

'Star?'

She was supposed to go out on a date last night. I popped by to get all the juicy details, since she wasn't at school today.

She's been looking forward to this since she met Rudy last week. She met him through another boy she knows at St Gustav's, so we don't know much about him. Except that he's quirky and good-looking and really makes her laugh. We stalked his Instagram together, looked at all his pictures, trying to decide what he was into. There were lots of cute pictures of him with his dog.

'What happened? Did he stand you up?' I ask.

'I guess what happened was what he expected to happen.'

'What do you mean?'

She rolls her eyes to the ceiling. 'Use your imagination.'

I picture various scenarios. Rudy humiliated her. He made fun of her outfit. He dropped her for another girl.

'What?'

'He attacked me,' Star finally says. 'He wouldn't take no for an answer.'

'You mean...he tried to...'

'Not tried to. Did.'

'No!' This weird, empty ache spreads through me. It's like my brain refuses to process what she's saying, like it's stuck or something. I can't—won't—believe it.

I fall back onto her bed. I feel like my head is going to explode. How could this happen and Star is still sitting here, eating cake and drinking tea? Why doesn't she have a black eye or a bandaged head or something?

'Did you tell your mum?'

She shakes her head. Star's mum is never home, anyway. She works three jobs. She's often out overnight, and asleep all day. That's one of the reasons I like coming over. I like the freedom. Star gets to do what she wants. She doesn't have to answer to anyone. She gets to eat toast for dinner, and stay up as late as she likes. Her mum doesn't mind.

Or doesn't care, says a tiny voice at the back of my head.

But this... this is one of those times you need a grown up. Someone's got to do something.

'You can't let him get away with this. You have to go to the police.'

Star shakes her head. 'My family doesn't go to the police. You know that.'

'You should post something on Instagram,' I suggest. 'Let everyone know what a sleaze he is.'

'No!' She shakes her head. 'I'm not putting myself out there. It's not worth it.'

She has a point. You make an accusation, and you soon find yourself in the firing line. I remember it happening to a girl in the year above us. She was attacked by two boys. She spoke up, and now her name is mud.

It seems too unfair. That Rudy should have done this and Star has to deal with it. Anger bubbles up inside me.

Star reaches for the knife she used to cut the cake with, her fingers curling around the handle. 'Maybe I should just finish myself off. Then I don't have to think about it anymore.'

'Don't say that,' I blurt, my heart racing. I keep my eyes on her, trying to work out if she's serious or if she's being dramatic.

She sets the knife down after a moment, and relief floods through me. Still, I wait until she goes to the toilet before slipping it into my bag. Just in case.

Mum rings to tell me to get home for dinner. It's so embarrassing, the way she does that. Why can't she just text like a normal person? But that's mums for you, I suppose. I reach for Star and give her a quick hug. Her arms hang loose around me like she's already somewhere else in her head.

I told Mum I wouldn't be late, but by the time I've got my shoes on, it's already quarter past. I suppose I could just cut through the park. If I do that, then my house is just another fifteen minutes. It should be fine.

I walk to the end of Star's road and cross over to the entrance of the park. It's a bit creepy, the way the trees blow about in the wind, but there's barely anyone around.

I'll be fine.

Star's secret feels like a boulder, crushing my chest, and I can't shake the image of her lying awake all night, dealing with that. I'm not looking for trouble. That's the last thing on my mind. But when I see Rudy Callaghan walking up the path towards me, my heart rate skyrockets. I can't stop myself. I ball my fists in fury. I'm fully prepared to walk past him, but when he calls out my name, my fight or flight instinct kicks in.

It's him or me.

FORTY-TWO
TAYLOR

Then

RUDY IS LOOKING AT me, his brown eyes meeting mine in what can only be described as a provocative manner.

'Taylor, isn't it?' he purrs. 'Fancy seeing you here. Star's told me all about you.'

I stare at him, shocked by his nerve. Who the hell does he think he is?

He reaches for me with one hand. He isn't rough, but I feel a bolt of electricity as his fingers brush my arm. I glance about. There's no one around. I try to step around him, but he follows.

'What's your hurry? Can't you stop and talk for a minute? I'd really like to get to know you.'

My heart is hammering. I'm actually shaking. I can't believe he's got the nerve to talk to me after what he did to Star.

Then I remember the knife I took from Star's house. I slip my hand into my pocket and feel the weight of it. It's good to have it there. Slowly, I withdraw it. Rudy's still talking. Mainly about himself. He tells me he's saw me playing cricket last year, and my team is good, but not as good as his.

'Maybe you and I should get together. I can give you a few pointers.'

He wiggles his eyebrows suggestively, and that's all it takes to tip me from sane to unbalanced.

'Get away from me!' I warn him. I change directions, crossing the path and moving towards the pond.

He takes a step closer. 'Come on, Taylor. You don't mean that. You're not like all the other girls. I...'

I look at his arrogant, entitled face. Someone needs to teach him a lesson. Him and all the other boys who think they're God's gift.

The world slows to a crawl as I push the sharp blade through the tender flesh of his stomach. My hand trembles as I pull it out, not daring to look at the damage I've caused. Rudy collapses to the ground with a gurgled cry, blood gushing from the wound.

He looks at me, not with lust, but with horror.

I panic, running as fast as I can to get away from him, away from the scene of my crime.

I keep going until I come to a water fountain just inside the gate at the other end. I stop and wash my hands. I've left Star's knife behind, I realise. I must have dropped it as I ran away. It'll have Rudy's blood all over it.

And my DNA.

I don't want to, but I force myself to head back up the path to where it happened. As I do, I see there is already a crowd gathering around him. He's been brought out onto the footpath, and a group of joggers are tending to him. One of them is holding what looks like a sanitary pad against the wound, but his shirt is covered in blood. There's a woman of my mum's age holding his hand and talking to him, another one on the phone to the emergency services. They're all doing everything they can to help him, but he's just looking at me. I don't know if he can see me, or if I imagine that he's locked me in his gaze. I see the knife lying off to the side and start towards it but someone stops me.

'Better not touch that, love. Leave it for the police.'

'Of...of course.'

I turn away, noticing for the first time that there is blood on the front of my shirt. I zip up my jacket, but no one is even looking at me. I quietly walk away.

All evening, I wait for the doorbell to ring. I think someone must have seen me. And if not, Rudy must have told them it was me. I check online and see reports of a young man being attacked in the park. The reports say his condition is critical and his family is at his bedside.

And yet I am still shocked when I see the news in the morning.

Rudy Callaghan is dead.

Star sees it too. She whispers the news to me in the playground. I thought she would be pleased, but instead she looks upset.

'I did it for you,' I tell her.

'Y..you killed Rudy?'

She looks at me like I'm a monster. I stare back at her. 'I thought that you, of all people, would be pleased.'

'No, Taylor!'

She backs away from me. And it's then the realisation hits me.

'He didn't attack you, did he? You made it all up.'

She doesn't deny it. I stare after her.

'Why did you do it, Star? Did he stand you up?'

She chokes back a sob. 'I waited all evening in that cafe. Everyone was looking at me. It was so humiliating. I just wanted him to know how that feels...'

My mouth fills with bile.

I attacked an innocent boy, and now he's dead. All because of her lies.

I will never, ever speak to Star Simpson again.

FORTY-THREE
JOY

I SIT AT THE top of the stairs and listen to Taylor talking, spilling her guts to Howard. At first, I feel a prick of jealousy that she has chosen him and not me. She always was a daddy's girl, even when she was small and sweet. But as she as unloads her story, my jealousy turns to shock.

I am stunned and horrified. I think of Rudy's poor mother, and his sisters. No wonder the Callaghans hate us. She killed their brother. I don't know how they know, when the police don't, but it seems they are the kind of people who prefer to take the law into their own hands.

And now they have Clara.

I shake with fury.

I can't hold back anymore. The anger and fear boil over, and before I know it, I'm barging into Taylor's room. She's sitting on the edge of her bed, her face streaked with tears. I glare at her, my voice trembling with fury.

'This is all your fault,' I snap. 'You've got to do whatever it takes to make this right. You've got to get Clara back.'

My words hang in the air, sharp and cutting, and I know I'm hysterical, but I can't stop. The thought of what Taylor has done, of how far things have spiralled, is too much. I knew she was going through a rebellious stage—what teenager doesn't? But murder? That's so far beyond anything I could've imagined that it hadn't even crossed my mind.

Taylor looks up at me with wide, tear-filled eyes, and for a moment, I see something in her expression: fear, guilt, maybe even regret. But it's not enough to cool the fire inside me.

Howard is shaking his head slowly.

'Joy, this isn't helping,' he says, his voice calm but firm, like he's trying to rein me in.

My fury shifts to him in an instant. His calm, measured tone only fuels my anger, and in that moment, I resent him for being so weak.

'Stop defending her!' I shout, my voice cracking under the strain. 'How do you...'

A sound cuts me off. Movement from downstairs. My heart leaps into my throat.

'Clara?'

I don't wait for an answer. I bolt down the stairs, the adrenaline coursing through me too fast to think. Behind me, I hear Howard and Taylor scrambling to follow, their footsteps pounding as we race to find out who—or what—it is.

'Clara?' I fly from one room to the next, but there's no one there. I race to the door, panic driving me forward. There's no time to put on my boots. I fling the door open and sprint out into the garden, the icy ground soaking through my socks with each step. I don't stop until I reach the gate.

I scan the lane, desperate for a glimpse of whoever it was, but there's no sign of anyone. Whoever was here has gone.

The adrenaline fades as I turn back toward the house, my shoulders heavy with defeat. I walk through the door, and peel my sodden socks off my feet and drop them onto the radiator.

Howard walks towards me.

'They left something,' he says quietly, leading me into the kitchen. On the table sits a small camcorder. The kind we used to use before we had smartphones.

'What's that for?' Taylor asks, though I'm sure she must know the answer.

Howard looks at her. 'They want you to record your confession.'

FORTY-FOUR
JOY

HOWARD PICKS UP THE camcorder carefully, as if it might explode in his hands. Beneath it lies a small slip of paper. He unfolds it, his brow furrowing, and tilts it so I can see.

PRESS PLAY.

Our eyes meet, and an unspoken wave of dread passes between us.

I watch as he jabs at the buttons with trembling fingers. The camcorder whirs to life, its tiny screen lighting up with a dim glow. We huddle together, our faces inches from the screen.

At first, the image is a mess of static and blurred shapes, almost unrecognisable. My breath catches as the camera adjusts, sharpening into focus.

Clara.

She's right there. Her small frame fills the screen. My heart twists at the sight of her. Tears blur my vision as I drink her in—my baby, my sweet girl.

Howard fumbles with the volume, turning it up too high before quickly dialling it down again. The blast of sound makes us flinch, but nothing could distract me from Clara.

She's outside in the snow, shivering violently, the wind tugging at her hair. She's not wearing a coat, just her pyjamas and boots. She has her arms wrapped tightly around herself as if she's trying to conserve what little warmth she has left.

I scan the screen, desperate for a clue as to where she is, but the landscape is barren. She stands alone in a wide expanse of snow. There are no houses, no fences, no power lines. The snow is pristine, undisturbed except for the small, uneven patches around her feet. Behind her, the mountains rise in jagged slopes, their sides heavy with snow that merges seamlessly with the flat grey sky.

Her teeth chatter audibly, the sound cuts through the static like a knife. Then she looks directly at the camera, her wide, terrified eyes locking onto mine.

'My name is Clara Applewood,' she says, her voice trembling. 'I am six years old. And I want to go home. Taylor, only you can help me. Please, please make a video, telling everyone what you did.'

She pauses, her breath visible in the icy air. The camera lingers on her as she hugs herself tighter, her lips blue from the cold.

We sit frozen, barely breathing, as the seconds tick by. Clara doesn't speak again for a long time, but the camera doesn't move. It just stays on her as she shivers, her small body trembling with every gust of wind.

Finally, she whispers, so softly we almost miss it, 'Please Taylor, help me. You're the only one who can.'

The video cuts out abruptly, leaving us staring at the now-black screen. For a long moment, none of us move. The silence in the room is deafening, broken only by the faint hum of the camcorder.

Howard doesn't look at me, and I can't tear my eyes from the screen, as if willing it to flicker back to life and give us more. But there's nothing. Just the haunting image of Clara burned into my mind.

There are tears in Howard's eyes. He wipes them away. 'She said she was six.'

'Yeah, I noticed that.'

We both look at Taylor.

'If I confess, I'll go to jail,' she says.

'You'll be fine. You're just a child.' I say.

It's a barefaced lie, but I can't worry about that right now.

Howard mumbles in agreement. He can't bring himself to say the words, but he too knows it's the lesser of two evils.

We both look at her, willing her to make the right decision.

FORTY-FIVE
CLARA

Four Hours Earlier

I can't breathe.

The sock in my mouth is scratchy and wet, pressing hard against my tongue, choking me with its bitter, horrible taste. It's all I can think about. My jaw aches from trying to push it out, but it won't budge. My nose is blocked, and every breath is a struggle.

Emily tumbles out of my bag into the snow, but no one notices. I try to cry out, but the sock muffles everything, pressing deeper into my throat. It's like it's growing, filling every part of my mouth. I want to spit it out, but I can't.

Rough, icy hands grab me, shoving me onto a sledge. The cold hits my legs, but the sock is all that matters. It's choking me, making my body ache. I try to twist it free, but powerful arms hold me tight, locking me down as the sledge jerks forward. We're flying downhill, bouncing and sliding over the snow. The sock is stealing every bit of air I can get through my nose.

Tears sting my eyes, and I squeeze them shut. My head is spinning. I try again to scream, but it's just a muffled sob against the damp, scratchy fabric. The taste of dirt and sweat makes me want to puke, but I can't.

The sledge screeches to a stop, and I'm yanked off and dragged forward. The sock rubs against my tongue, making my throat burn and my head pound.

One of the girls lifts me onto her shoulders. I hate being close to her, but it's easier to breathe up here. I can see for miles—fields, trees, and the white slope behind us where the cottage should be. It's gone now, hidden by the hill. I try to call for Mum, but all I can do is moan.

I spot a bright orange bus in the distance. It's just like the one we took pictures of outside that pub the other day. For a moment, hope flickers inside me. If I can get there, someone will help me. I try to fight, kicking my legs, twisting in the girl's grip, but she hauls me down like I weigh nothing. Her hands are strong and cold as she shoves me forward, forcing me to stumble through the snow, gasping through my nose.

I see people on the bus. I wave to them, wanting them to help me, but as we get closer, I realise they are Callaghans. Their faces are hard, watching us through the windows. This is their bus. This is where they're taking me.

The door opens and I want to scream, to beg for someone to stop them, but the sock chokes me, stuffing every sound back down. I stumble as they push me inside, my feet sliding on the icy step. And the door slams shut behind me.

FORTY-SIX
CLARA

THE INSIDE OF THE bus looks like a squished house. On one side, there's a tiny kitchen with a crooked cupboard and a little stove. Along the walls, there are saggy sofas with mismatched cushions. One has stuffing spilling out of it. Shoes and clothes have been shoved underneath the sofas like they were kicked there in a hurry.

The floor is dirty, with food wrappers and crumbs scattered across it. The curtains are green, the colour of bogies and they're too thin to block out the light. The whole bus smells like damp clothes and vinegar. My mouth aches so bad. I start to pull the sock out, but one of the big girls notices. She slaps my arm away, and tears spring to my eyes.

'Sit!' she snaps, pointing to a spot on the floor.

I do what she says, sliding down until I'm leaning against the soft seat. My body aches, and my jaw is locked, but I don't dare fight back. The girls all talk loudly, laughing and smiling like they've done something amazing. They're so pleased with themselves, like this is the best game ever.

I listen hard, hoping to catch something useful, something that might help me escape. But their words are jumbled, buzzing like bees. My head feels heavy, and the room spins. Tiny white dots dance in front of my eyes, and their voices sound far away, like they're underwater.

I close my eyes. There are six of them, and only one of me. I work out that the meanest one is Angel. She steps on my foot on purpose as she walks past. Pain shoots up my leg, and I curl my toes, biting back another muffled cry.

I hate her.

I want her to die.

I want them all to die. But I want her to die the most.

The youngest one, the one they call Adelaide, shoots me a quick, worried look. For a second, our eyes meet, and I think she might say something, but then she turns away, like she's scared of getting caught. She walks to the little kitchen area and opens the fridge, pulling out a packet of sausages.

I watch her hands as she works. The sausages are all linked together in a string, shiny and pale. She separates them with a pair of scissors, cutting each one apart with quick snips. Then she drops them into the hot pan on the stove. The sausages sputter and pop, and the savoury smell drifts around the bus.

My eyes water. My stomach growls, and I curl my knees up to my chest. I can't swallow properly, and the salty taste of it mixes horribly with the delicious smell of sausages. No one is paying me any attention, so I duck my head down and yank the sock out of my mouth, coughing as I gulp in the fresh air. My hands shake as I stuff it into my pocket and wipe my mouth on my sleeve. My throat is sore, but I can finally breathe.

I watch as Adelaide flips the sausages over with a fork.

'Ready!' she calls, and the others shuffle forward, grabbing sausages and buns, smothering them in ketchup. Not one of them even glances at me. My tummy twists with hunger, as they gather around the table, laughing and eating like everything is normal. To them, I'm not even human. Just a thing. Even pets get fed.

Angel glances at me, her eyes sharp and mean. Then she licks her lips slowly, smirking as she takes a big bite of her hotdog. She chews deliberately, making a show of how much she's enjoying it, her gaze never leaving mine.

I think about my family. They must know I'm gone by now.

Mummy will be angry, and Daddy will call the police. They'll put these girls in the worst jail ever, with slimy walls and gross, mouldy food and a toilet that stinks so bad they can't even eat. And when they're locked up, I'm going to visit them and eat marshmallows and M&M's right in front of them. I smile a little at that and glance out the window. I wonder how long it will be before they come?

When the girls finish eating, Adelaide scrapes the leftovers onto one plate and heads for the door. I watch closely as she unhooks the latch.

'Kingsley!' she calls out, cupping her hands around her mouth. 'Here, boy!' She waits for a moment, then comes back inside, frowning. 'I can't find Kingsley.'

Angel barges past Adelaide, shoving her roughly aside. 'Kingsley?' she yells, her voice sharp and mean. 'Where are you, you stupid mutt?'

Adelaide's face flushes red, and I hear her say something under her breath.

The other girls stomp outside, their boots crunching loudly in the snow. And now it's just me and Adelaide. I look out the window. I can see them all, heading off in different directions, calling for the dog.

Adelaide goes to stand by the door. Her chin quivers. I think she's worried about her dog.

I realise I'm still wearing my backpack. I shrug it off and reach inside. I take all the dolls out and lay them in front of me. One, two, three...

'How old are you? Six?' Adelaide says.

I nod my head. People often think I'm younger than I am. It normally bothers me, but right now it might be a good thing. If they think I'm only six, they won't realise how clever I am.

'I'm ten. I don't play with dolls anymore,' Adelaide says.

I'll still be playing with dolls when I'm twenty, but I don't tell her that. She's not my friend.

I brush the dolls' hair, tying it back and switching their clothes around until they all look right.

One looks like Mummy. One looks like Daddy. And the other one is Taylor.

The other girls come back in, slamming the door behind them. They are arguing with each other about who was supposed to be looking after Kingsley.

'Brooke's the one who let him out,' someone says.

'Adelaide was supposed to look after him.'

'Adelaide's just a kid.'

Angel comes over to me and stares right in my face. 'You're a cool one,' she says. 'Adelaide would be bawling her eyes out in your place.' She looks over at her youngest sister and laughs.

Adelaide looks insulted.

'Leave her alone', says the one with the thorns on her collarbones. Ivy, I think she's called.

'Water?' I croak.

Angel ignores me, but Ivy fetches me a glass. I drink it down quickly. It tastes a bit yucky but I'm too thirsty to care. Once I've finished, I clutch the glass in my hand. Glass is dangerous, Daddy's always telling me that. You have to be really careful you don't smash it because the little pieces are really sharp.

As sharp as knives.

The girls are all arguing over whose fault it is the dog ran off. No one is watching me. I bring the glass down hard on the table. When it doesn't break, I lift it again and slam it down with a big clunk. I freeze, wondering if anyone heard, but they are too busy arguing to notice. I look down at the glass. There's a big crack down the middle. I do it again. Bits of glass fall onto the table like crumbs.

Oh, my hand's bleeding.

I don't want them to see, so I sweep the pile of glass under the table, all except the biggest piece, which I slip into my pocket. Then I wrap my hand with the sock. It's sore and bloody but I don't tell anyone. I don't want them to know.

Adelaide walks over, holding out some colouring books and pens.

'Thought you might want something to do,' she says, avoiding my eyes as she puts them down in front of me.

'Thanks.'

I pick up a pen and start colouring. I feel my shoulders relax as I colour in a Christmas tree. I've always liked colouring. It's relaxing. I finish the tree and pick up a red pen to colour the presents. Then it occurs to me that I'm too good. If I were six, I'd be terrible at this. Deliberately, I start scribbling outside the lines, making the picture look messy and childish.

Adelaide leans over to peek at my work. 'That's quite good,' she says.

It isn't. I can do much better. I don't say anything, just keep scribbling.

Under the table, my left hand is clenched tight around the glass shard. Blood trickles slowly through my fingers and down the sock wrapped around my wrist, dripping onto the floor. I try not to wince or look down, I just keep colouring – badly - pretending everything's fine.

The other girls have fallen silent. They are talking in low voices as if they don't want me to hear. Then Ivy turns and looks at me.

'When can I go home?' I ask.

She tilts her head. 'We need your sister to do something for us first.'

'What?'

She studies me for a moment. 'Actually, we're going to need you to do something too.'

'Okay,'

I don't care what it is. I just want to go home.

'Brave little thing, aren't you?' Ivy says.

'She doesn't really know what's going on, does she?' Angel says.

She grabs one of my dolls from the table. 'I need to borrow this.'

I get an ache in my tummy, but I pretend not to care.

'You can have this back when you've made the video,' she says.

I nod.

'I need the toilet first,' I say. I squirm about, like I can't trust my bladder.

I'm six, remember. I might wet myself.

'Adelaide, can you take her? Don't forget to use the cuff.'

Adelaide walks over to me and clips a bracelet onto my right arm. It's on a chain, attached to another bracelet, which she clips onto her left arm so that we're cuffed together. Then she leads me outside.

'You can go behind that tree over there,' she says.

I nod. I thought there was a toilet in the van, but I don't question it. Even though it's cold out here, I'm glad to have the chance to get outside. I test out the cuff. It's tight. I can't get it over my wrist. I look a little closer and see that there's a little keyhole.

Damn!

I glance over at Adelaide. It looks like the only way I can escape is if I can convince her to come with me.

'Don't look', I say, as I bend down to wee.

I look down at my hand. It's stop bleeding now. I peel off the sock and stick it in my pocket. Then I check to make sure I still have the shard of glass. I find it, and pick it up between my finger and my thumb.

'There are a lot of you, aren't there?' I say to Adelaide.

'We're a big family.'

I could stab her with this, right in the neck.

'Where's your Mummy?'

'At home. Probably drinking. That's all she does.'

'My mummy drinks too.' I say.

She looks interested so I keep talking. 'She drinks wine after work, especially on the weekend. Daddy drinks too.'

Adelaide shakes her head. 'It's not the same thing. My mum doesn't work. She just drinks all day, until she passes out. That's all she does.'

I squat lower. It's almost impossible to wee in this cold. I don't want to get it down my leg.

'So it's all sisters?' I say. 'You haven't got any brothers? I haven't either.'

Adelaide is looking at me with a weird expression on her face.

'Time's up,' she says, yanking on the cuffs.

I swallow hard. 'You can let me go. Just undo the bracelet. You can say it came off.'

'No!' she growls.

I pull up my trousers. The hems are wet from the snow.

I look up into the mountains, hoping to see a flash of lights. Where are the police cars? The helicopters? What's taking them so long? They've got radars and police dogs and all sorts. Why aren't they coming for me?

Then it hits me. Everything closes for Christmas. Shops, schools, even the swimming pool. What if the police are on holiday too? What if no one's coming for me?

I glance at Adelaide. She's the only one who's been remotely nice to me, but it doesn't matter. She's still part of this. She's still keeping me here. My hand tightens around the shard of glass in my pocket. I could hurt her, but I'd still need the key.

The bus door slides open again. The other girls jump out one after the other, their boots clomping on the floor. Quickly, I shove my hand deeper into my pocket, hiding the glass. My chest tightens as Angel strides toward me, her eyes fixed on mine.

A fresh wave of fear surges through me. I force a smile. 'Can we go sledging again?' I ask, my voice wobbling just a little.

Angel snorts, like I've just told the silliest joke in the world. She crouches down in front of me. Her face so close I can smell the ketchup on her breath.

'Clara, it's time,' she says, her voice is cold and steady.

'Time for what?'

Angel's smile spreads slowly across her face, slow and cruel.

'You'll see.'

FORTY-SEVEN
CLARA

'GIVE ME YOUR COAT,' Angel demands.

I slip the glass shard into my jeans pocket, then shrug off my coat and hand it to her. She tosses it to the floor, then unclips the cuffs and grabs my hand. Her grip is rough, and her eyes flick briefly over the blood on my palm. She doesn't say anything. She doesn't care.

We trudge out into the snow, Angel leading the way. Ivy and another girl I don't know the name of follow close behind. The cold bites through my clothes, making me shiver. My nose and ears tingle. The snow is wet and slushy as we walk farther away from the bus.

Finally, Angel stops and turns to face me. 'Right, Clara. You're going to make a video.'

For a moment, I feel a spark of hope. A video? This I can do.

'I want you to say your full name and then you're going to ask Taylor to make a video confessing to what she's done.'

I blink, confused. I have no idea what she thinks Taylor has done, but this shouldn't be too hard. Taylor loves making videos. She and Star used to have their own YouTube channel. Their videos weren't great, mostly them giggling and telling jokes about things I don't understand, but Taylor always had fun with it. She won't mind making another one, I'm sure.

As Angel fiddles with her phone, I ask, 'Why did you take my coat?'

She glances up at me with a smirk. 'I want them to see we're serious.'

That makes no sense to me. They've already kidnapped me. Isn't that serious enough?

Angel makes me record the video over and over. Each time, she finds something wrong with it. I think she's just looking for reasons to be mean. She yanks me by the arm, dragging me into a new spot. 'Stand here. No, not like that, you idiot!' she snaps, shoving me into place. 'Look at the camera, not at the ground. Are you stupid?'

She glares at me every time I mess up, her eyes cold and angry. 'Stick out your lip more. You're supposed to look sad, not bored.' Her voice is sharp, and it makes my tummy twist every time she speaks. 'Say Taylor's name properly! Like you care about her. God, do I have to teach you everything?'

I try my best, but my brain has turned to ice-cream. I'm so cold I can barely think straight. My teeth are chattering so hard I can hardly get the words out. Snot is dripping down my face, and I can't stop it.

'Ugh, you look disgusting,' Angel snaps, wrinkling her nose. 'Stop snivelling. No one's going to feel sorry for you like that.'

My trainers are soaked, and my toes are completely numb. I don't know how much longer I can stand here in the freezing cold, but Angel doesn't care. She just keeps shoving her phone in my face and barking orders.

'Again. And this time, try not to screw up.'

FORTY-EIGHT
CLARA

I'M BACK ON THE bus, sitting on the sofa, clutching a mug of hot chocolate. My fingers and toes tingle like mad as they defrost, and every movement sends sharp, prickly pains shooting through them. I squirm, trying to hide how much it hurts. Ivy is sitting across from me, leaning forward, her elbows on her knees. Her expression is serious, but there's something in her eyes that looks almost... sad.

'You deserve to know the truth, Clara. About what your sister did.'

I nod, my throat tight. I don't think I want to know anymore, not really, but it feels too late to stop.

'I hadn't even heard of Taylor until the night our brother died,' Ivy begins.

My fingers tighten around the mug, the warmth doing little to stop my shivering. I don't say anything. I just wait.

'We got a call out of the blue, telling us to get to the hospital. They told us Rudy had been stabbed, and he wasn't expected to last the night. Can you imagine what that was like?'

I shake my head, fresh tears prickling in my eyes.

'When we arrived, he was in a terrible state. We were only allowed to see him for a few minutes to say goodbye.' She pauses, swallowing hard. 'I was the last to go in. I took his hand. I could already feel the life draining out of him.'

My tummy aches, and I clutch the mug tighter, wishing it could block out her words.

'I said, "Who did this to you?"' Ivy's voice cracks slightly, but she presses on. 'I didn't expect him to reply, but all of a sudden, he looked at me. And with his last breath, he said, "Taylor. Taylor Applewood."'

My mind reels, spinning so fast it feels like I might fall off the sofa. I stare down at my lap. Ivy looks serious, but her words don't make sense.

'No,' I whisper, shaking my head. 'Taylor isn't like that. She would never stab someone.'

Ivy's mouth tightens into a thin line. 'Well, apparently she did. A friend of mine saw her in the park that night. So we know she was there.'

I shake my head again, but this time it's slower, less certain. We aren't even allowed to go to the park at night. Bad things happen there. Everybody knows that. Taylor wouldn't break that rule. Would she?

I glance at Ivy again. She's picking the paint off her nails, her fingers working quickly, like she needs to keep busy.

'After Rudy died, we couldn't let it go,' Ivy says, her voice harder now. 'I started asking about her, and someone told me she was friends with a girl called Lucy Charlton.'

'I know Lucy,' I say softly, my voice barely a whisper.

'We caught her outside the Riverwood shopping centre,' Ivy continues. 'At first, she lied, said she didn't know Taylor. But when she saw she was outnumbered, she backed down. She told us the address, and that was that. We could've gone to the police with what we knew, but I wasn't sure it was enough.' She pauses, her eyes narrowing slightly. 'I know in my gut that Taylor killed Rudy. All I really want is a confession.'

Her words hang heavy in the air, and I can feel the weight of them pressing down on me.

'So your sister has a choice to make, Clara,' Ivy says, her voice cold and sharp. 'Does she love herself more than she loves you?'

I stare down at my lap, my hands shaking as I grip the mug. I don't know what to say. I don't know what to think. I just wish I knew the answer.

FORTY-NINE
JOY

'YOU HAVE TO DO this,' I say. 'You saw her. She'll catch her death out there.'

'We can rescue her,' Taylor says desperately. 'The snow is starting to melt. We can get in the car and drive it further down the road. We can find her.'

'The roads are still very icy,' Howard says.

'We don't have time,' I cut in. 'She won't last long in the cold. You need to do it now, Taylor.'

'Please!' Howard chips in. 'For Clara.'

Taylor sits there for a moment, a dark frown on her face, then shakes herself. 'I'll do it.'

Howard throws his arms around her. 'Good girl.'

I can't even look at her. I still can't believe she stabbed that boy. I don't think I'll ever get over it.

I draw a breath.

'If you can take care of the video, I'll have another go at getting help,' I say. 'I don't think it's safe to go by car yet, but I can try again on foot.'

'Thank you,' Taylor says.

But I'm not doing it for her. I'm doing it for Clara.

I head to the door and begin pulling my boots on.

'We'll get her back,' Howard calls after me.

I think about the way they've strung this out, the slow agonising torture they've reaped upon us. There's absolutely nothing in their behaviour that makes me think they'll keep their side of the bargain.

I find a piece of string and tie it to Kingsley's collar.

'Come on, I need you,' I tell him.

I walk Kingsley as far as the lane, then let him take the lead. His nose is low to the ground as he follows the road towards the place where I found Emily. I can't tell if he's picking up a trail or just taking the easy route, heading downhill.

The sun breaks through the grey sky, casting a warm glow over the snow. It's a welcome reprieve, and for a moment, the world looks softer, the snow sparkling like scattered diamonds. Kingsley and I keep moving, further down the hill than I went last time. According to the map, there's supposed to be a shop about half a mile from here. If I can find it, maybe they'll have a phone and I can call the police.

The thought spurs me on, even as the walk grows harder, the snow slick underfoot. I keep my eyes on the trees and fields, scanning for any sign of life—smoke from a chimney, a car, anything. But all I see is white and grey. The world seems empty around me. And I get this feeling, like this is the end of days.

I try not to think about Taylor and what she's done. The weight of it presses against my chest, but I shove it aside, focusing instead on Clara. Is she scared? Crying? Or worse, has she already...

No. I shake my head, forcing the thought away.

Don't think about that.

But the dark thoughts sneak in anyway, quiet and relentless, like blood seeping from an open wound.

The road forks ahead. One path winds deeper into the valley, the other climbs uphill. Kingsley tugs on the lead, urging me forward. But as I take my first step, my foot skids on an icy patch, and I crash hard onto my side.

The impact steals the breath from my lungs, leaving me gasping. I let go of the lead and my phone flies out of my hand, skittering across the frozen ground.

'No, no, no!' I scramble after it, my fingers trembling as I grab it. The screen is cracked, jagged lines slicing through the glass. My stomach twists. I look around. Kingsley hasn't moved. He's looking at me, wagging his tail. Tears sting my eyes and I pat his fluffy head. I shove the phone into my pocket and pick up the lead, forcing myself to keep moving. The snow deepens with every step as I descend, the cold biting at my legs as it rises up to my calves.

Then I see it.

A wall of snow, thick and towering, blocking the road entirely.

I reach out and touch it. The surface isn't soft or powdery. It's rough, jagged, like crushed glass frozen in place. The cold stabs at my fingertips, the edges biting back.

Someone built this.

I raise my foot and kick at the wall, my boot slamming into the ice. Cracks spread out like tiny lightning bolts, but the wall holds firm. Frustration bubbles over, and I kick again. And again. Sweat trickles down my neck, and my breath clouds the air as I pound against it with everything I have.

It's no use. The wall isn't going anywhere. My legs ache, my chest burns, but I refuse to stand still. Gritting my teeth, I scoop Kingsley up into my coat, and start to climb. The ice is uneven, slick in some places, jagged in others. My boots slip and slide, forcing me to steady myself with shaking hands as I struggle upward.

When I finally make it to the other side, I land awkwardly in the snow. My coat is drenched and I am shivering uncontrollably. The cold feels sharper now, cutting through the wet fabric, straight to my skin. But I keep going.

The road is clearer here. Someone has scraped the snow away, leaving faint tracks behind.

I follow them, my breath puffing in short bursts, the cold air stinging my lungs.

Finally, a building comes into view, its outline stark against the vast, snowy landscape. My chest tightens with hope, and I break into a run, pushing past the burning ache in my legs.

There's a shop, just as I'd hoped. But when I reach the door, I find it locked. A handwritten sign taped to the frosted window stops me cold:

Gone to Skye for Christmas. Back in the New Year.

I stare at the sign for a moment, disbelief coursing through me. Then, desperation takes over.

'No!' I cry, slamming my fists against the glass. 'Help! Someone call the police!'

The sound of my shouting rings out, echoing through the valley. It's eerily quiet here, the kind of silence that feels alive. The mountains rise on either side, their snow-covered slopes casting long, pale shadows. The wind cuts through the air, sharp and unforgiving, and I can hear it whistling faintly through the trees in the distance.

The valley stretches out endlessly, its white expanse broken only by the narrow line of the road behind me. There's no movement, no sounds of life. Just the relentless silence of the wilderness, closing in around me.

I want to keep searching, but I'm so cold and exhausted. Maybe it would be better to head back to the cottage and get warm. I'm standing there, deliberating with myself when I hear footsteps. And a moment later, a teenager jumps down from a tree. I turn towards her eagerly, when I realise it's one of the Callaghans.

Angel, if I'm not mistaken. She sees me too. Her face is half-hidden under her scarf, but it's definitely her, the girl I fought with last night.

'Well, look who it is,' she says, as if we are old friends.

My stomach tightens, and I grip Kingsley's lead.

She gestures towards the shop. 'Looks like we're both out of luck.'

I take a step towards her. Force myself to look her in the eyes.

'Angel,' I say, my voice trembling slightly. 'Please. Where is Clara?'

Her smirk widens, cruel as cold porridge. 'Wouldn't you like to know?'

'Please, she's just a little girl. She doesn't deserve this. Let her come home.'

Angel lets out a short, harsh laugh, shaking her head. 'Home?' she sneers. 'With a family of killers?'

I shake my head quickly. 'Clara has nothing to do with any of this.'

'She's leverage.'

Tears prick at my eyes, and my chest feels like it's caving in. 'I'll give you Kingsley,' I say, desperation spilling out.

Angel stares at me for a moment, then throws her head back and laughs, loud and harsh. 'Kingsley?' she says, wiping an imaginary tear from her eye. 'That stupid mutt? I've never liked him.'

I feel my knees go weak, the rejection hitting me like a blow. 'Please,' I whisper, my voice cracking. 'I'll do anything.'

Angel tilts her head, her smirk fading slightly as she studies me. Then, with a slow, deliberate step forward, her cruel smile returns.

'I'll give you Clara,' she says, her voice soft but icy. 'If you give me Taylor.'

The words knock the air out of me.

'You're out of your mind!'

Angel's smile widens, cruel and knowing. 'Am I? Seems like a fair deal to me. One kid for the other. Bring her here at five and we'll do a swap.'

I can't speak. My heart is beating so fast I can barely hear.

Angel leans closer. 'But I'm telling you, this is a one-time offer. If Taylor is not here by five, you'll never see Clara again. And that's a promise.'

'You're insane,' I whisper,

But she just smirks at me. 'Their lives are in your hands.'

FIFTY

JOY

WHEN I RETURN, THE air in the cottage feels tense, charged with an unspoken energy. Taylor is sitting at the table, arms crossed, her blonde hair pulled back in a messy bun. She looks up as I step inside.

'It's done,' she says flatly.

I nod. 'Good.'

Howard stands nearby, his arms folded tightly across his chest. 'Do you want to watch it?' he asks.

I shake my head quickly. 'God no.'

Taylor huffs, leaning back in her chair. 'What are we supposed to do with it now?' she asks, frustration creeping into her voice. 'There are no instructions on the note. Do you think they're going to come back for it?'

I glance at her, my heart tightening. She looks so young in this moment, her defiance tempered by a flicker of fear she's trying to hide.

'Actually, I ran into one of the Callaghans while I was out,' I say, keeping my tone as steady as I can manage.

Both Taylor and Howard turn to look at me.

'What happened?' Taylor demands to know.

'I tried to swap Kingsley for Clara,' I say, my cheeks burning with shame even as I speak. 'But she wasn't interested.'

Howard's eyes narrow.

'But she said to come back at five,' I add quickly, filling the silence. 'I suppose they want the video, then.'

Taylor's jaw tightens, and she glances away. Howard doesn't say anything, but I can feel his gaze on me.

Heat creeps up my neck. I haven't even made my decision yet; I tell myself. I'm just setting the groundwork. But the guilt swirls in my stomach.

'I'm going to go and take a shower,' I say, turning away before they can press me further.

I hurry upstairs, my footsteps echoing in the quiet house. When I reach the bathroom, I shut the door behind me and lean against it, my chest heaving. I can't face her right now, Taylor, with her fierce eyes and that stubborn tilt of her chin. If I look at her too long, I know I'll cave.

How can I be expected to choose between them?

Taylor might be the difficult one, the rebel, the one who pushes the boundaries to their limits. But she's still my daughter, and I love her with all my heart.

But do I love her more than Clara?

The thought hits me like a punch, and I bury my face in my hands. I can't believe this is happening. I can't believe they're forcing me to choose.

FIFTY-ONE
JOY

WE'VE GOT A FEW hours yet.

I dress quickly and head back downstairs. 'I think we should get back out there and clear the road as far as we can. I want to drive down to the meeting place. That way, if they bring Clara, we can grab her back.'

'If they even bring her,' Howard says. He's uncharacteristically pessimistic. But who can blame him? Who knows what they're going to do.

We bundle up, grabbing whatever we can find—shovels, brooms, even a dustpan—and step out into the cold. The snow is thick and heavy, clinging stubbornly to everything. Howard and I get to work, while Taylor trails behind us. She is still not quite recovered from her injury and it shows.

Howard leads the way, the scrape of his shovel loud against the frozen ground. I fall in beside him, brushing away at the snow with my broom. Taylor follows a little slower, using a spade to break apart the packed snow.

The work is brutal; the cold numbing my fingers even through my thick ski gloves. I focus on the rhythm of the task—the scrape of metal, the crunch of snow, the way the sun is peeking through the clouds, offering the faintest warmth.

Is Clara still outside, I wonder? Have they at least given her a coat? It scares me how cold she looked in that video. But it just goes to show how deliberately cruel the Callaghans are.

We work for hours, clearing the lane inch by inch. Taylor barely speaks, her breath visible in the freezing air, but her movements are purposeful, each shovelful of snow flung aside with an angry force. I want to say something, to comfort her, but I can't find the words. This is not a scenario you read about in parenting books.

What do you say when your child has murdered someone?

I still can't find the words.

My mind keeps drifting to Clara—sweet, innocent Clara. I dig harder, throwing everything I have into the task. We keep working until we reach the snow wall. I hack at it angrily, feeling a burst of triumph as our combined efforts break it down.

When the snow is finally cleared, we step back to inspect our work. The grit glistens faintly in the sunlight, and the road looks passable now, though how much further we'll get, I'm not sure.

'There,' Howard says, his voice tight with exhaustion. 'That'll have to do.'

Taylor nods, her face wet with sweat and tears, but for once, she doesn't complain.

We trudge back to the house and warm up again, psyching ourselves up for our appointment. Taylor sits at the kitchen table, shoulders slumped, staring at the floor. My heart twists painfully.

She's just a child. How has she carried this enormous burden all alone? How did she not break under the pressure of it?

But then my thoughts turn to Clara. My bright, lively little girl. She has her whole life ahead of her. Taylor made a choice. Clara didn't.

I try to push the thought away, but it lingers, dark and ugly.

Guilt washes over me, bitter and suffocating. I press my fingers to my temples, trying to force my thoughts into order, but my mind is a chaotic mess of anger, blame, and fear.

I think about the confession. Taylor's right. If this gets out, her life is over. She's looking at serious jail time if the police take it as seriously as I think they will.

But Clara, Clara is still so young. Her life is only just beginning.

I picture her face, her smile, the way she clings to her dolls like they're her lifeline. My fists clench as I imagine her scared, cold, and wondering why we haven't come for her.

I need some air.

I go to the window and pop it open, then stand there gripping the counter. The room feels too small, the air too thick.

A boy is dead, killed by my daughter.

Nausea rises in my throat, hot and choking, and I bend over the sink, gasping until it passes. My chest aches, my tears falling freely now.

I have to choose.

There's no good answer. No way out.

I glance at the clock. It's time to go.

I head outside and start the engine, gathering my thoughts while I warm up the car. I watch as Taylor and Howard walk towards me. I take in every detail of Taylor's face as she climbs into the car. She sits silently in the back and stares out the window. Her face is pale, her hands clenched tightly in her lap.

'Let's get Clara back,' I say, more to convince myself than anyone else.

I put the car into gear and we coast slowly down the drive towards our fate.

FIFTY-TWO
JOY

THE ORANGE VW RUMBLES into view, its worn tires crunching over the snow-packed road. My heart lurches as the doors open and four of the Callaghan girls climb out. Angel leads the way, her head high, a smirk already forming on her lips. Behind her, the youngest girl shifts uncomfortably, her eyes darting to the ground as though she doesn't want to be here.

I run towards the van, desperate to find Clara. I see someone sitting in the driver's seat, their hands resting casually on the steering wheel, but the curtains behind them are drawn and I can't see in.

The Callaghans block my way before I can get to the door. I stop short, turning to look at Howard. He's standing a few paces back, his hands raised slightly in a placating gesture. He's here to negotiate, not to fight.

I turn back to Angel, and we come face to face.

'Where's Clara?' My voice is hoarse with fear and desperation.

Angel's smirk deepens, and her dark eyes glitter. 'She's safe.'

My fists clench at my sides. 'I need to see her,' I say, through the tightness in my throat. 'I need to know she's alive.'

The youngest girl shifts again, her shoulders hunching as she looks at the ground. When her gaze finally lifts to meet mine, it isn't cold or defiant—it's afraid. For a moment, my anger wavers, replaced by confusion.

Angel's gaze moves past me to Taylor, her expression hardening with undisguised hatred.

'Have you made the video?'

Taylor nods stiffly, her jaw tight.

'I can't hear you!' Angel barks.

'It's done,' Taylor spits, her voice sharp and defiant. There's a fire in her eyes I haven't seen in a long time.

'Bring it to me.'

Taylor glances at me briefly before stepping forward. My stomach churns as I watch her move. Each step feels like a countdown to disaster.

I see a flutter of movement. My heart leaps into my throat as Clara's face appears at the window, her hand lifting to wave. Relief surges through me, but it's fleeting. Another Callaghan is behind her. They are watching us. Watching Taylor.

Clara is so small, so fragile. She needs me. Taylor is strong, resourceful. Maybe... maybe she could survive this.

The rationalisation slithers into my mind, unbidden and monstrous.

Taylor will fight.
Clara wouldn't stand a chance.

'Good choice,' Angel says, her gaze flicking to me.

It doesn't feel like a choice at all.

Taylor hands over the camcorder. Angel snatches it without so much as a thank-you, her attention already shifting. The van door creaks open, and the oldest Callaghan steps out, pulling Clara with her.

'Mummy!' Clara cries, her voice high and desperate.

The Callaghan girl keeps a firm grip on her hand as they approach. My heart pounds as Clara is brought closer. So close I can feel her fear.

'We've done what you asked,' I say, my voice trembling.

Angel and another girl grab Taylor by the wrists.

'Hey!' Taylor yelps, her voice rising in surprise. She struggles, kicking and twisting, but she's too weak to put up a fight.

Angel nods to the oldest Callaghan, signalling to her to release Clara. But just as she does, the girl screams.

It happens so fast I almost miss it. Clara twists free, and there's a flash of movement, something sharp and glinting in the weak light. Blood spurts from the older girl's neck, and I realise with horror that Clara has attacked her. The older girl has a shard of glass embedded in her throat.

Clara runs toward me, her tiny legs moving faster than I've ever seen.

'Mummy!'

I catch her, pulling her into my arms. I hold her tight as her little heart pounds against mine. Relief crashes over me in waves, but it's short-lived.

'No!' Taylor's voice rings out, sharp and panicked.

I turn to see Angel and the others shoving her toward the van. Taylor fights back, shrieking and kicking, but they overpower her.

'No!' I scream, my voice raw. 'No!'

Howard sprints toward them, but as the van roars to life, he's shoved backward into the snow. The van lurches forward, its tires skidding on the icy road.

I let go of Clara and chase after it, screaming Taylor's name, my boots slipping in the slush. The van picks up speed, its taillights fading into the distance.

I drop to my knees in the snow, my breath heaving in my chest. Clara clings to me, her sobs echoing in the stillness, but all I can see is Taylor's terrified face.

FIFTY-THREE

JOY

HOWARD SCRAMBLES TO HIS feet, snow clinging to his clothes. He's running after the van now, banging on the windows with his fists. His shouts echo into the cold air.

'No!' I scream after them, my voice hoarse. 'Come back!'

I scramble to my feet, my heart hammering in my chest as I sprint towards our car.

'Get in!' I shout to Howard and Clara, throwing myself into the driver's seat. Clara is sobbing, her little face buried against Howard's chest as he jumps in behind her.. The engine roars to life, and we're off, tearing down the icy road.

This is one fight they are not going to win.

'I'm coming, Taylor!' I yell into the windshield, my voice raw and full of fury. I mean it. I cannot—*will not*—let them take her.

Howard sits in the back with Clara, holding her tight, whispering words I can't hear. My focus is locked on the van ahead, its taillights glowing dimly through the slush that sprays up from its tires.

The roads are a mess, the snow and ice churned into slippery slush. The tires slide with every sharp turn, the car threatening to fishtail out of control. The mountains loom ahead, their paths narrow and treacherous. There are sheer drops on either side, plunging into darkness, but the orange van doesn't slow down.

'They're going to kill her,' I mutter under my breath, my grip tightening on the steering wheel. The thought sends a jolt of adrenaline through me.

Howard leans forward, his voice urgent. 'Joy, slow down! The road...'

My eyes burn as I focus on the van, pushing the car faster. The engine whines, the tires struggle to grip.

The van veers around a bend, its wheels skidding dangerously close to the edge. I follow, my heart pounding so hard it feels like it might burst. Every second that passes, every inch they gain, feels like another nail in Taylor's coffin.

I can't let them win. Not this time.

FIFTY-FOUR
JOY

THE ROAD AHEAD IS a mess of slush and mud. My knuckles are white on the steering wheel as I navigate the narrow, winding descent toward the valley. Howard sits with his hand clamped on the door handle as if it will steady him. His jaw is tight, his eyes fixed on the road ahead.

'Careful,' he warns, his voice tense. 'The roads are...'

'I know!' I snap, cutting him off. My nerves are fraying with every second, my pulse hammering in my ears. I can't afford to lose focus. Not when Taylor is counting on me.

'There!' Clara shouts from the back seat, leaning forward between us. Her small finger points to a faint glow in the distance. Red taillights.

My heart leaps. 'Hold on!'

I press my foot down on the accelerator, and the car lurches forward. The tires struggle for traction on the wet road, skidding slightly, but I don't ease off.

Up ahead, the orange van is weaving erratically, its back wheels sliding dangerously close to the edge of the road. The Callaghans are driving too fast for the conditions, and I feel a wave of dread rise in my chest. If they lose control...

'Don't let them get away!' Clara cries.

'I won't,' I say through gritted teeth. But how am I supposed to stop them?

The van takes a sharp turn up ahead, disappearing from view. My heart leaps into my throat, and I press the accelerator harder.

'Mummy, hurry!' Clara shouts, her voice breaking.

'I'm trying!' My hands tremble on the wheel.

We round the bend, and the taillights come back into view, closer now. The road ahead narrows, bordered by steep drops on one side and a wall of thick pine trees on the other. The cliffs loom in the distance, jagged and menacing against the darkening sky.

The van jerks wildly, swerving as the driver tries to keep control. Their driving grows even more erratic, the back fishtailing on the slick road.

I catch a glimpse of Taylor through the back window. Her face is pale, her expression hollow, eyes haunted. For a moment, I think she's looking right at me, and guilt sears me. She knows. She knows I handed her over.

The road twists sharply, the guardrails are missing where other vehicles have skidded off the edge. My stomach churns as the van veers dangerously close to one of the gaps.

We are just behind them now. My racing instincts kick in, my years behind the wheel sharpening my focus. I know how to handle roads like this. They don't.

The van hits a patch of slush and fishtails again, the back end swinging wildly toward the cliff's edge. My breath catches as the driver fights to correct it.

Then it happens.

The van tilts sharply to one side, its momentum carrying it toward the edge. For one agonising moment, it hangs there, balanced precariously.

'No!' I scream, my voice raw. 'Taylor!'

The van tips.

I watch as it goes over the edge, crashing down the rocks. The sound is deafening—metal twisting, glass shattering, the van slamming against the cliff face.

I slam on the brakes, and the car skids to a halt, just short of the cliff's edge.

The world is silent, except for the sound of my own ragged breathing.

'Mummy?' Clara whispers, her voice trembling.

Howard grips my arm, his face pale. 'Joy...'

I don't respond. My eyes are locked on the spot where the van disappeared, and I scream Taylor's name over and over.

FIFTY-FIVE

JOY

I LEAN MY HEAD on the dashboard.

It's over, and we've all lost.

A scream pierces the air.

'Help!'

I wrench the door open and step out. I look over the ledge and see Taylor clinging to a rock a few metres down.

My incredible, brave girl.

'Mum!' she cries, her voice cracking with terror.

'I'm coming! Just hang on!'

The rocks are slick, the ground unstable, but none of that matters. My focus is all on Taylor.

I find a foothold and begin to climb down. It's amazing the way the rocks have formed against the edge of the cliff here. Almost like steps. I climb carefully, knowing at any moment it could all give way. The steps stop a little way above Taylor's head. I lean down and reach for her. Our fingers touch. I let out a breath and stretch my body further.

'I've got you!'

Her skin is ice cold, her grip weak, but I hold on.

'I'm not letting go,' I promise, my voice firm despite the fear coursing through me.

I barely register the movement nearby. It's Angel, dangling from another rock. I don't even look at her.

All my attention is on Taylor.

'Hold on!'

Howard is climbing down too. When he reaches the bottom of the steps, he slips his arms around my waist so I don't fall. I plant my feet against the slick ledge and hang down. I glimpse the van as it sinks into the loch below. Such a long way down. I can't think about that now. I hold on to Taylor and pull with all my might.

Taylor cries out as I lift her. I drag her higher and she trembles as she reaches the ledge. I pull her up, until she is lying beside me, her eyes wide with shock.

'You're safe now,' I whisper, holding her tight. Her face presses against my neck, her breath coming in shallow gasps.

Together, we help her up the steps. When we reach the top, I collapse beside her onto the wet ground.

I gather her in my arms, her body trembling against mine. Her eyes are still glassy.

'I knew we weren't going to make it,' she says. 'So I jumped out of the van.'

'You're an incredibly brave young woman.' I kiss her damp forehead. 'Don't worry, you're safe now.'

She shakes her head. 'I'm broken, Mum. I'm all broken.'

'You'll be okay,' I promise her. 'Everything will be okay.'

Behind me, I hear movement. Howard has returned to the ledge.

'Angel's still down there. I'm going to go back and help her.'

'Howard, no!'

I don't want him risking himself, especially not for her.

But he's already gone.

FIFTY-SIX
HOWARD

EVERY STEP FEELS PRECARIOUS as I lower myself back down onto the ledge. I look down and see Angel. She is crying softly, as she clings to the edge of the rock, her fingers are bloodied from the effort of hanging on, her face is streaked with dirt and desperation.

'Help me!' she cries. Her voice is raw and pleading.

I inch closer. The cold air is sharp in my lungs. She looks up at me, her dark eyes filled with fear.

'I can't hang on much longer.'

I climb down slowly. Little rocks fall as I make my descent. It's strange. Usually I don't like heights, but all my fear has vanished. I'm just so elated to have Taylor back, Clara, too. I didn't think we would survive this Christmas. I truly thought it was the end.

I look down at Angel. She seems so small, clinging to the rock face. Her eyes brim with tears and it's hard to imagine she's the same teenager who caused my family so much grief. She looks so pathetic and helpless. I reach for her hand, steady and deliberate.

'Not long now,' I call down to her.

'H...hurry.'

One by one, I peel her fingers away from the rock.

Her relief changes to confusion. 'What...what are you doing?' she shrieks, her voice climbing in panic.

I meet her gaze. My heart is steel.

'No!' She scrambles to get a better hold on the slippery rock. 'Please! Don't do this!'

It's too late. I'm already prying the last finger loose.

Her scream pierces the air, and I watch as she falls, spinning down, down, down.

I shudder as her body slams against the rocks on the way. When she hits the bottom, I don't even hear the splash. I watch for a moment, satisfied that all is calm and still.

I give her a little wave.

'Goodbye, Angel.'

Some people just can't be helped.

FIFTY-SEVEN
JOY

HOWARD RETURNS ALONE, HIS face pale and drawn. I don't ask him what happened, and he doesn't offer an explanation. I assume he failed in his rescue mission, but I don't care. I'm just glad he's back.

'How's Taylor doing?' he asks.

Taylor is stretched out on the back seat, her head resting on Clara's lap. Her face is ashen, her breathing shallow, and she groans softly and Clara strokes her hair gently, whispering words of comfort, but I can see she's worried.

'She's in pain. We need to get her to a hospital.'

Howard slides into the passenger seat, and I grip the wheel, driving away at a much slower pace than before. The recklessness of earlier is gone, but the roads are still treacherous, demanding every ounce of my attention.

Twice, the car gets stuck in the slush, and each time, Howard and I have to get out to dig the tires free. My hands are numb by the time we manage to push through the worst of it. The bigger, clearer roads ahead feel like a lifeline, and as we hit them, I allow myself a breath of relief, finally able to pick up speed.

The silence in the car is heavy, broken only by Taylor's occasional whimpers.

'We must have coverage by now. Should we call the police?' I ask, glancing at Howard.

He shakes his head. 'There won't be any survivors,' he says flatly. 'We need to concentrate on getting Taylor to the hospital.'

I nod, gripping the wheel tighter. He's right. The Callaghans are gone. They're no longer a threat. Taylor and Clara are all that matter now.

The drive to the hospital passes in a blur. My hands tremble against the wheel, my heart pounding as the image of the van plunging over the cliff plays on a loop in my mind. We came so close to losing her.

Too close.

The hospital comes into view, its harsh lights piercing through the gloom. I pull into the emergency bay; the tires skidding slightly on the slick pavement. Before the car has even come to a complete stop, Howard is out, flagging down a nurse.

She takes one look at Taylor—her pale face, the faint rise and fall of her chest—and feels her weak pulse. Her expression hardens with urgency, and she disappears inside without a word. Moments later, she returns with a wheelchair.

Taylor groans faintly as Howard and the nurse lift her from the back seat. Clara clings to her hand until the last possible moment, tears streaking her face as she follows them inside.

I sit frozen for a beat, gripping the wheel as I watch them go. Then I force myself to move. The car needs to be parked, and I need to be with Taylor.

It feels like hours, but it's only minutes later when I walk through the hospital doors. The bright lights and antiseptic smell hit me all at once, disorienting me after the long drive. I find Howard and Clara in the waiting area.

'Where is she?' I ask, breathless.

A doctor approaches us, her expression professional but kind. 'We're prepping Taylor for surgery,' she says. 'There's significant concern about her spine. We need to act quickly to prevent further deterioration. She also needs a blood transfusion. She's lost a lot of blood.'

My breath catches in my throat. My legs feel unsteady, and I lower myself into a nearby chair.

'Is she going to be okay?' I manage to ask, my voice barely above a whisper.

The doctor hesitates. 'We're doing everything we can. She's young, and that's in her favour.'

Clara climbs into my lap, clutching her doll tight. I wrap my arms around her, drawing comfort from her small, trembling form. Howard sits beside me, silent, his hands clasped together as if in prayer.

A little later, we move to a bigger waiting area where there are books and toys for Clara, but she just slumps in a seat and falls asleep on my shoulder.

'I'm going to pop back to the car to check on Kingsley,' Howard says. 'Do you want me to get you anything?'

I shake my head and hold Clara a little tighter. Her sleeping body feels hot and sweaty in my arms, just like when she was a baby.

Howard returns a little later and hands me a coffee I didn't ask for.

'There's a little something in there to calm your nerves,' he says.

'Thank you.'

I take a sip. He's right. It's just what I need.

For a while, we sit in silence. When he finally speaks, his voice is low:

'Let's not tell the police.'

I understand what he's saying. There's nothing to be gained by telling the whole truth. We've got our family back. And the Callaghans are at the bottom of the loch, as is the camcorder. The evidence is gone. The nightmare is over.

We've survived.

We just need Taylor to pull through, and then we can finally move on.

FIFTY-EIGHT
JOY

I JERK AWAKE. I don't know how long I slept for. I don't know how I *could* sleep. The waiting room is so uncomfortable. Howard is asleep too, sleeping with his mouth wide open.

'Mummy?' Clara's voice drags me back to the present.

'Yes, sweetheart?'

'Is Taylor going to be okay now?'

'I don't know,' I admit, my voice cracking.

Howard's hand brushes my arm, grounding me. 'She's strong, Joy. She'll pull through.'

I nod again, but his words don't ease my guilt.

I can't stop the flood of memories: Taylor, as a baby, clutching my finger with her tiny hand. Her first steps, tearing around Aunt Dorothy's living room. I think of all the times she's made me laugh with her clever, dry wit. I think of her as teenager, pushing every boundary I set. Then I think of her walking over to Angel with the camcorder, not knowing she was walking into a trap.

The guilt claws at me, sharp and unrelenting.

'I betrayed her,' I whisper, my voice barely audible.

Howard looks at me. 'What are you talking about?'

"I told her we were going to save Clara, but I'd already made a deal with Angel: Taylor for Clara. I betrayed her.'

His expression shows shock, but then softens. 'They put us all in an impossible situation. You had to do what you had to do.'

'I had a choice.'

I look down at Clara, playing with Emily on the floor, and swallow back the tears.

A doctor strides into the waiting room.

'Taylor Callaghan?' she calls.

I leap to my feet. 'That's our daughter.'

She nods, her face kind but professional.

'The surgery went as planned, and I'm pleased with how everything went. We were able to stabilise the affected area without any complications. We'll be monitoring her recovery closely, but all the initial signs are positive.'

'Oh, thank god.' Howard and I hug each other.

'We'll keep a close eye on her pain management and mobility in the coming days, and the physiotherapy team will work with her to help with her rehabilitation. If you have any questions or concerns, I'm happy to go through everything in more detail.'

'Can we see her?' I ask.

'You can go in now if you like, but just for a few minutes.'

I swallow hard. 'Thank you so much.'

The relief is overwhelming, but it's tangled with guilt. I glance at Howard, who nods, urging me forward.

Taylor looks fragile, swallowed by crisp white sheets and surrounded by wires and blinking machines. Her fiery spirit has been dampened, her pale face slack, her chest rising and falling with shallow, uneven breaths.

I ease into the chair beside her and reach for her hand. Her fingers are limp against mine.

'I'm so sorry,' I whisper, my voice breaking as hot tears roll unchecked down my cheeks. 'For everything. For not protecting you. For letting it come to this.'

Her hand twitches, the faintest response, but enough to pull a sob from my chest.

'You're going to get better now. I love you so much.'

Her eyelids flutter, lashes trembling against her pale skin, and then she looks at me. Her voice is barely a whisper. 'I know, Mum.'

FIFTY-NINE
TAYLOR

I sit up in my hospital bed, the card from my class resting on my lap. It's one of those oversized ones, with a cartoon puppy on the front. Everyone's scribbled something, some of it genuinely sweet, but most of it just lame jokes. I roll my eyes at the doodle someone's drawn. It looks like a cricket bat with legs, but when I see Star's signature, my throat tightens.

Miss you so much x

Her words bring tears to my eyes. Despite everything, I miss Star too. I stare at the card, feeling the raw ache of longing. Maybe, one day, we could be friends again. But for now, it feels too soon. If only she hadn't lied, I wouldn't have made the biggest mistake of my life.

Rudy's face flashes through my mind. I will never forget him. I'll never forget what I've done. Even if I'm not arrested, I'll have to live with it for the rest of my life.

That's my prison sentence.

I look up and see Mum and Dad coming onto the ward, with Clara trailing behind. She's clutching a new doll. This one has red hair and a fishtail.

'Your tooth fell out,' I say, staring at the gap in her smile.

Clara nods. 'The tooth fairy left me a tenner.'

'A tenner?' I raise my brows at Mum, but Clara doesn't notice.

'I bought this doll in the gift shop.'

She holds it out to me to admire.

'Her name is Thunder.'

'Nice.'

She leans closer. 'She spends a lot of time in the gym, so she has major upper body strength, and I'm making her body armour.'

'I wouldn't mess with her.'

Clara nods, satisfied.

I look over her head at my parents. Dad has his arm wrapped protectively around Mum's waist. It's kind of gross, to be honest, but at the same time, it's good to see them like this. Maybe what happened has brought them closer together.

I hear more voices, and to my surprise, it's Lucy and Bess. Bess bounds ahead like a dog, her energy filling the sterile room. Lucy follows, clutching a notebook.

'We missed you!' Bess chirps, planting herself on the other side of my bed. 'When are you going home?'

'Hopefully in a week or two,' I say. 'I'll be stuck downstairs, though. Mum and Dad are turning the study into a bedroom for me.'

'That's cool,' Bess says, swiping one of my grapes. 'You'll be right by the snack cupboard.'

'Exactly,' I say with a wink.

Lucy opens her notebook, showing me sketches of dance routines she's been working on. I glance through them, swallowing the sting of jealousy. It'll be months before I'm able to do anything like that. And the cricket season is a write-off. But I force myself to nod appreciatively.

'I'm going to work towards my coaching qualifications,' I say, trying to sound upbeat. 'That way, I can help from the sidelines.

Lucy fills me in on all the latest gossip. Miss Todd has got engaged. Mrs Dunstanburgh has been spotted working in Sainsbury's on the weekends.

'She's moonlighting,' Bess says, as if this is some kind of illicit activity.

'Star was asking after you,' Lucy says. 'She wondered if she could visit.'

I blink at her, caught off guard. The thought sends a lump to my throat. I nod slowly, not trusting myself to speak.

Clara grabs her new iPhone from her pocket and brings up a photo of Kingsley. She holds it out to Bess, who squeals in delight.

'He's gorgeous! Dad, can we get a dog? Please? I'll feed it and walk it every day!'

Gio looks horrified. 'I don't think we have room for a dog right now.'

'I want a dog!' Bess wails, throwing herself on the floor. She kicks her arms and legs so wildly that I half expect a nurse to come in with a syringe. Nobody pays her any attention. The adults look away and talk amongst themselves. Eventually, Bess gets bored. She opens my bedside locker and pulls something out.

'What's this?'

I stare at it. 'That's my...that's a hammer.'

Lucy darts a look at me. 'Why have you got that?'

'Actually, I think I might have accidentally brought it home from school. Can you do me a favour and return it?'

She looks at me oddly, but she takes the hammer and slips it into her bag.

'Right, Bess. I think we'd better get you home,' Gio says, looking relieved that the tantrum is over. For now.

I wave goodbye. I dread to think what Bess is going to be like when she's a teenager.

'Just us, then Pumpkin.'

Dad wipes his glasses on his tie and smiles round at Clara, Mum and me and I feel a twist of pleasure as I realise I'm getting my life back.

Well, almost.

SIXTY

JOY

A couple of months on, life is starting to feel a bit more normal. Today is my day working from home, but I'm taking a break to walk Kingsley after dropping the kids off at school. Today was also Taylor's first day back and I really hope it goes well. She's got a way to go, but the doctors are hopeful she will get her full range of mobility back eventually.

I walk Kingsley down past the shops. I've found a nice little café where I can grab a coffee and a Puppuccino for Kingsley. I never really thought of myself as a dog person before, but Kingsley has been good for me. I've become quite attached to him.

As I walk towards the café, I notice a woman staring at me. She is scruffy and dishevelled looking. Yet there is something familiar about her. We lock eyes as I cross the street and I realise with a jolt that it's the Callaghan's mum.

She looks at Kingsley, then at me, and her mouth falls open. I should stop and talk to her, but what would I say? Rightfully, I suppose Kingsley belongs to her, but how could I return him without explaining everything that happened? The girls died because of their vendetta against us, and if we hadn't taken him, Kingsley would have died with them.

I hurry on up the road and do not look back until I'm sure I've lost her. Much as I like that café, I'm going to have to find somewhere new to take Kingsley. Somewhere on the other side of town.

I head home and ring Howard, tell him what has happened.

'Don't worry, I'll sort it,' he says in that calm way of his.

'How are you going to do that?'

There's a pause.

'I'm going to go round there and tell her the truth,' he says.

'Oh, Howard. Are you sure?'

'Believe me, honesty is the best policy.'

I wish I could agree with him, but we have gone to such lengths to get our family back. What if she goes to the police, as she has every right to do?

'She won't tell anyone,' he says, as if reading my mind. 'The woman's a drunk, from what I've heard. Even if she decides to blab, the police are unlikely to listen. But for my own peace of mind, I think we owe it to her to tell her the truth. I'd want to know, wouldn't you?'

I swallow hard. I'm not at all sure I agree with him. But I can hardly stop him. Once Howard makes up his mind about something, he can be surprisingly pig-headed.

SIXTY-ONE
HOWARD

Three Months Earlier

I SIT BACK IN my chair and pull my glasses off, massaging the bridge of my nose. I've been staring at the screen all afternoon, numbers and graphs swimming before my eyes. The mug beside me is long since empty, a cold ring of tea at the bottom. I think about making another cup, but my phone buzzes before I can get up. Taylor:

> *Walking home from Star's.*

I frown, glancing at the window. The daylight is fading fast, a deep grey spreading across the street. I tap out a quick reply:

> *Stick to the streets, not the park.*

I know Taylor though. She'll cut through the park. She always does, no matter how many times I've told her not to. It's quicker, more direct, and she hates being told what to do. My stomach churns at the thought. I glance at my watch. Maybe I should stretch my legs. It's only a short walk, and I could do with some air.

The path is quiet when I arrive. A couple of joggers whizz pass me, their ponytails swaying in time with their steps. I give them a polite smile. Then a couple more people walk past, dogs sniffing the ground.

I cut diagonally across the open space, my breath misting in the cold air. My eyes scan the path ahead, searching for Taylor. I don't want her to think

I'm checking up on her. She'd never let me hear the end of it, but I can't help worrying. She's independent, headstrong, but she's still my little girl. No matter how capable she thinks she is, she's not invincible.

I hear her voice before I see her. It's sharp, with that edge she uses when she's annoyed. I slow my pace and duck behind a bush. She's talking to a boy—short, stocky, with a mop of black curls and deep, intense eyes that seem... off. There's something unsettling about the way he looks at her, his gaze is too direct, too invasive.

They step off the main path, disappearing into a more secluded area of the park. My stomach knots. What is he doing? Is he trying to get her alone? I edge closer, staying behind the bush, watching as they stop near a cluster of trees. Taylor crosses her arms, her stance defensive. The boy leans in, gesturing with his hands, his voice low and insistent.

I can't hear what they're saying, but Taylor's body language speaks volumes. She shifts her weight, glances over her shoulder, then takes a step back. My instinct screams at me to intervene, to step in and pull her away. But I hesitate. She's always telling me she can handle herself. Maybe I should let her prove it.

Then I see her reach into her bag. My breath catches. A second later, her hand emerges, holding a knife. My stomach drops.

The scene unfolds like a nightmare. The boy steps forward, his hands raised in a placating gesture. Taylor shouts something, her voice sharp, panicked. The knife plunges into his stomach, a quick, jerking motion. Both of them freeze for a moment, as if neither can quite process what's just happened. Then the boy stumbles back, clutching his abdomen. Blood seeps through his fingers, dark and glistening in the fading light.

Taylor gasps and drops the knife. She takes a step back, then turns and runs, her footsteps crunching on the wet ground.

I'm frozen to the spot, my heart hammering. The boy collapses to his knees, his breath ragged. He's clutching his stomach, trying to stem the flow of blood, but it's too much. Too fast.

I step out from behind the bush, my legs shaking. He looks up at me, his face pale, his eyes glassy with pain. He tries to speak, but all that comes out is a wet, gurgling sound.

The knife lies on the ground between us, its blade slick with blood. I glance at the boy, then down the path where Taylor disappeared. My mind races. She defended herself. She had no choice. But if he survives, he'll tell the police. He'll ruin her life.

I pick up the knife. It feels heavy in my hand, the handle slick. The boy's eyes widen as I step closer. He tries to crawl away, but he's too weak. I kneel beside him, my breath hitching in my chest.

'I'm sorry,' I whisper.

With a surge of adrenaline, I drive the knife into his chest. His body jerks once, then goes still. The only sound is the soft rustling of leaves in the wind.

I stand over him, my chest heaving. I watch him as I wipe the knife on my tie, then let it clatter to the ground. My mind is blank, a deafening roar in my ears. My legs feel like lead as I turn and walk away, back towards the path. Back towards home.

Taylor needs me to make this go away. You do what you have to do.

You protect your own.

SIXTY-TWO
HOWARD

THERESE CALLAGHAN'S HOUSE IS quiet as I step inside. I close the door behind me and glance around the room. It's modest, if a little run-down, with mismatched furniture and a faint smell of mildew.

She sits in the armchair by the window, her face pale and drawn. When she looks up at me, her eyes are haunted, rimmed with dark shadows, like she hasn't slept in days, maybe weeks.

'Thank you for agreeing to speak to me,' I say. 'I promise I won't take too much of your time.'

She looks at me with thinly veiled disgust. 'What are you doing here?'

'It's like I told you. I came to tell you the truth.'

Her gaze sharpens, her body tensing. She doesn't respond, just watches and waits.

I draw a breath and start. I tell her everything—about Taylor and Rudy, and how it all spiraled out of control. The words spill out of me, raw and unfiltered. I tell her about the way the girls treated us. How they took Clara, and then Taylor.

I explain how the van left the road. How we rescued Taylor but left Angel hanging. Taylor was right, it feels good to unburden myself. To confess.

Her expression doesn't change, but I see the tension building in her shoulders, the way her hands grip the arms of the chair.

When I'm finished, she looks at me like I'm a monster.

'Why are you telling me all this?' she asks.

'I can only imagine what it's like,' I say softly, my voice barely more than a whisper. 'To lose your children. To wonder what happened to them. To not know the whole truth.'

Her lips tremble. 'You've got a nerve, coming here. I know your type. You get a kick out if it, don't you? You get off on other people's pain.'

I take a step closer, my hand slipping behind my back. The cushion is there, soft and firm. My fingers close around it.

'I'm so sorry,' I tell her. 'For all of it. I want you to know it's nothing personal.'

Her eyes widen as I bring the cushion forward. She tries to scream, but the sound is muffled, lost in the thick fabric. Her hands claw at mine, weak and frantic, but I hold steady, pressing down.

I watch the clock on the wall. She loses consciousness after the first minute, but according to the statistics, this method of death takes three to five minutes. I go for five, just to be certain. It's a bit like boiling an egg. You don't want it too runny.

When five minutes have passed, I let the cushion fall to the floor and step back to review the results. I reach for her wrist and check for a pulse.

There is none.

Good. Job done.

Like I said, it's nothing personal.

You do what you have to do to protect your family.

I'm sure, under the same circumstances you would do the same.

AFTERWORD

Dear Reader,

Thank you for reading *The Christmas Present*.

I hope you enjoyed spending time with Joy, Taylor, Clara and Howard. This story is about the bonds of family, the weight of secrets, and the impossible choices we sometimes face. I hope it kept you turning the pages and questioning what you would do in their place.

At the centre of it all is Joy, who is forced to choose between her daughters in a way no parent should ever have to. Her love for Taylor and Clara drives her to unimaginable lengths, even as she grapples with her own doubts and guilt. Writing her journey, her moments of resilience, despair was a lot of fun.

Then there's Howard. On the surface, he's a good man, a devoted father and husband who would do anything for his family. Yet he is far more complicated than they realise. At times, his weakness and indecision frustrate Joy, and perhaps you too, as a reader. But what's most unsettling is the side of him that remains hidden. Beneath his mild exterior lies a darkness, a capacity for action that even those closest to him would struggle to believe. How far would he go for his family? And at what cost?

Taylor and Clara bring their own unique challenges and strengths to the story. Taylor's rebellious, sharp-edged guilt contrasts with Clara's innocent but perceptive courage. Together, they test the limits of Joy and Howard's love, pushing the family into the depths of danger and sacrifice.

And of course, the Callaghans. They are the looming threat, a family shaped by grief and revenge, who demand choices that no one should ever have to make. Their twisted sense of justice forces Joy, Howard, and their daughters to confront the worst in themselves and each other.

Ultimately, *The Christmas Present* is about the lines we draw between love and survival, loyalty and betrayal. It's about what we hide from those closest to us, and what happens when those secrets are dragged out into the light.

If *The Christmas Present* resonated with you, I would be so grateful if you could leave a review. Your feedback helps other readers discover the book and encourages me to keep writing.

To stay updated on future releases or just to say hello, visit LornaDounaeva .com or connect with me on Facebook. I'd love to hear your thoughts about the book - what surprised you, what moved you, and what theories you might have about these characters' futures. And if you want to share pet photos or your favourite Christmas traditions, I'm always happy to see them!

Thank you for taking this journey with me. I can't wait to bring you more thrilling stories soon.

Wishing you a very merry Christmas and a happy new year,
Lorna

Also by

Coming soon: The Perfect Daughter

More books by Lorna Dounaeva
The Beach
The Perfect Housemate
The Wife's Mistake
The Family Trap
The Perfect Family
The Wrong Twin
The Girl in the Woods
The Perfect Girl

The McBride Vendetta Psychological Thriller Series

FRY
Angel Dust
Cold Bath Lane
The Wedding (Short story)
The Girl Who Caught Fire
The Bitter End
You can find a full list of books at www.LornaDounaeva.com

About The Author

Lorna Dounaeva is a politics graduate who worked for the British Home Office before turning to crime fiction. She writes dark domestic thrillers and is especially fond of female villains. She lives in the Orkney islands with her Ukrainian husband and his parents, three children, a crafty cat and a happy dog.

You can contact her at info@lornadounaeva.com

Made in United States
Cleveland, OH
17 December 2024

12072181R00132